sex education

Club Radiant

emilia rose

To all my besties, who have low standards, like sweet, BDSM-loving billionaire boyfriends twice their age.

1

sierra

WITH HEAT GATHERED between my thighs, I teetered nervously from foot to foot in front of two muscular bouncers, dressed in all black suits, and chewed on the inside of my cheek. I shouldn't be here, but I had no other choice.

"Membership card," the bouncer with gold brass knuckles said.

"I, um …" I gulped. "Don't have one. I'm here to sign up for the class."

They peered at each other for a moment, then unhooked a maroon velvet rope barrier for me to pass. "Drop your coat off at the check-in and find your way down the hallway to the left to be received."

"Th-thanks," I stuttered. Heart pounding, I smiled softly and walked past the rope and through the double doors into Radiant, a BDSM sex club nestled in the heart of Pittsburgh that catered to the upper class.

Only problem was that I was a virgin with zero experience in sex and way too poor to afford any type of membership to this place. But Radiant was infamous for hosting proper Sex Education classes that not only taught *how* to do it, but also the mannerisms behind it all.

Vanilla drifted through my nose, and I peered past the coatroom and into the club, eyes widening when I spotted a bunch of naked women dancing around shiny stripper poles while onlookers watched from black suede couches.

"Your coat, miss," a woman said.

I shrugged off my jacket and handed it to her. She glanced down at my oversize baby-blue sweater with red mushrooms on it and a pair of leggings that might've had a hole near my inner thigh.

Why had I come here again?! I didn't fit in at all.

After grimacing, she placed my belongings in the back and pointed down the hallway to the left. With my arms crossed, I walked down the hallway and tried *not* to look into the glass rooms where men and women bound each other up.

Did they … know that these were glass walls and that anyone could look right in?

As the man plunged into the woman from behind, he grasped her hips and looked directly at me, a smirk crawling across his handsome face. I inhaled sharply. More heat grew between my thighs, my panties already soaked.

Scurrying along down the hallway, I desperately tried to gather my thoughts. The hallway opened up into a larger bar area. I stopped at the entrance and nervously glanced around, not sure where to go. Was I supposed to be in an office? Did the classes start tonight in those glass rooms and I was just late?

God, I hoped not. I couldn't imagine doing something like *that* in front of other people.

I glanced toward the bar and spotted a handsome older man with streaks of salt in his dark hair. He leaned against the counter next to two others with a drink in his hand and his devilish eyes fixed on me.

When he pushed himself off the bar, I wanted to look away, but I was fixed to the spot. Dressed in navy suit pants and a blue dress shirt with its sleeves rolled up his muscular forearms, he smirked and stopped in front of me.

"Can I help you?" he asked, his voice deep and British.

"I, um …" I whispered, the accent flustering me. "Maybe? I'm looking for the offices."

"The offices?"

My cheeks flushed, and I averted my gaze. "To sign up for a class. There was …" Somehow, my cheeks burned even hotter. "There was an advertisement online about a Sex Education course that this club hosted. But, um … maybe I'm just in the wrong p-place."

"God, you're fucking adorable."

I snapped my eyes up to meet his.

D-did he just …

No. No, I am hearing things. This music is way too loud.

"What?" I asked for clarification because if I didn't, my dumbass would nod along and get myself into a situation that I really, really didn't want to be in, like I had with Luke. I'd learned my lesson that night.

He leaned down and brushed some hair behind my shoulder, his lips dangerously close to my ear. "Which class are you interested in?" he asked, his voice smooth, *soft* almost, which made my nipples ache.

Get ahold of yourself, Sierra.

But everyone around us was kissing, grinding against each other, or fucking in the middle of the club. And I couldn't keep my damn head straight anymore. This was better than any porn I had ever watched.

"Th-the beginner course."

He dropped his hand to my waist, his touch respectful—though I wished it were anything but.

"The what?" he hummed.

I gently placed my hand on his muscular shoulder and stood on my tiptoes to reach his ear. "The beginner course," I said, desperately trying to control myself. But his body heat was making this room unbearable. "I'm supposed to see Michelle to sign up."

My mouth dried. God, he was the most attractive man I had ever seen.

I looked away so I wouldn't blush again and to push all this hotness out of my mind. He was way out of my league and looked like a regular at this club. And if he *was* a regular, why would he even want to be with me, Miss Clueless?

"Are you taking the class for a reason?"

"My ... friend said that I should."

"Your friend?"

"My ex-boyfriend," I whispered, loathing the thought of how he had made me feel that last time I was with him.

Technically, we hadn't officially broken up, but he'd completely ghosted me after pressuring me into giving him a blow job, which he called, "The worst blow of my life."

"Ah, there it is." He chuckled, the sound doing something to me. "Always the boyfriend."

"No, it's me. I'm not good at any of thi—" I started but cut myself short because why the hell was I talking about my sex life with a random stranger?! He didn't give a shit what I was good at or not. He was just showing me to the office.

"It's not you," he said. "A lot of men don't know how to treat a woman in the bedroom."

"Or out of it," I murmured to myself. *Stupid Luke.*

After a moment, he slid his hand onto my lower back and guided me through the crowd. Women threw me dirty looks, looking me up and down like I was trash. And I mean, I was definitely dressed that way. I didn't have money like these people.

We walked to a set of stairs that led to a second floor, where it was a bit quieter and I could hear my thoughts.

"Interesting choice of clothes for a sex club," he noted once we made it through the crowd.

"Oh," I whispered, cheeks flushing. Apparently, they were perpetually pink now. "I just came from my classes at college. I didn't have much time to change. I mean, I could've gone home to change, but I don't like staying out too late by myself, and, um … now, I'm oversharing."

I giggled nervously and played with the end of my sleeve.

Damn, why am I so awkward?!

We walked down another hallway filled with more of those glass rooms, but the people inside these were … doing even raunchier things with whips, weapons, masks, and more. I widened my eyes and peered up at him, catching him watching me.

"Do you like it?" he asked.

"What?"

"Knife play."

"Kn-knife play," I repeated because I feared that I hadn't heard him correctly. When he nodded, I swallowed hard and glanced back into the room. "I don't know what that is. I-I barely know how to give someone a blow job." The words tumbled out of my mouth before I could stop them. I slapped a hand over my mouth and stared up in horror at the gorgeous man in front of me, feeling so embarrassed that I couldn't even give oral correctly.

But also that I'd just admitted it out loud!

"There's no reason to be embarrassed about that, Miss …"

"Monroe. Sierra Monroe."

"Well, Sierra"—he stopped in front of a door and extended his hand—"I'll make sure we fix that during class. I'm Steven Patton. Your new professor."

2

steven

"Y-YOU'RE THE PROFESSOR?" Sierra asked, eyes widening. "F-for the course?"

A smirk tugged at the corner of my lips. "Yes."

"Oh my God," she said, hiding behind her hands. "I'm so sorry."

After a chuckle left my lips, I placed my hand on her lower back and steered her in the direction of the main office, where she could officially sign up for Sex Education 101. Michelle was the organizer for every class, and she had roped me into teaching this time after giving me a sob story about how we needed to help more people.

"There's nothing to apologize for, Miss Monroe, was it?"

"Sierra. You can call me Sierra. But there totally is! I just—" She smacked her lips together and averted her gaze. "You know what? I'm, um, going to shut up now before I say something I shouldn't."

"I'd love to hear all the things you shouldn't say," I murmured.

Cheeks turning a shade darker, she peered back up at me through her lashes and cracked a small smile. I stopped to catch my breath and gathered my thoughts before pausing in front of Michelle's office.

I knocked three times. "Michelle!"

"Come in, Steven," she hummed.

Once I pushed the door open, I allowed Sierra to step into the room and then followed her. A waft of strawberries drifted from her hair. She stopped in front of Michelle's desk and smiled nervously.

"You must be Sierra," Michelle said, extending her hand. "I'm Michelle Patton."

Sierra formed an O with her mouth. "Oh, a-are you two married?"

"Michelle is my sister," I clarified.

"Adopted sister," Michelle added. "That's why we don't look anything alike."

Sierra nodded, then glanced back at me—or more specifically, my bare left hand. "Oh."

"You're here to enroll in Sex Education?" Michelle asked.

Sierra nodded.

Usually, at this point in the conversation, I'd leave and let Michelle do her job. But I found myself shutting the door gently to give Sierra privacy and sitting on the maroon couch in Michelle's office.

"Great!" Michelle said, taking note. "We have one spot left."

"Lucky, lucky, Miss Monroe."

"So very much," she whispered, playing with the end of her sleeve and peeking another glance up at me. With her breath sucked in just a smidgen, she inched her legs closer together and returned her gaze to Michelle. "Is there anything you need from me?"

"Yes." My sister handed her a clipboard. "Please fill out the information and sign."

Sierra sat on the edge of the couch beside me while Michelle leaned back in her seat and smirked in my direction. I stared back blankly, not wanting her to make a big deal out of this once Sierra left. I'd bet this was the exact reason she wanted me to teach.

Five minutes of silence later, Sierra stood and handed the clipboard back to Michelle, who reviewed it briefly for a signature. She unclipped the papers and filed them in a cabinet. "You're all set, Sierra. Here are some papers to explain the class in more depth."

"Great," Sierra said, blushing. "I will, um, see you soon then, Professor."

"Don't be late for class, Miss Monroe," I said. "We start tomorrow night."

She paused at the door, holding the stack of papers to her chest and blushing again—which was going to drive me mad throughout the semester. I didn't know how long I'd last with her sitting up front, staring at me with those huge brown eyes.

"I won't be," she said shyly.

Michelle leaned back in her swivel chair as Sierra scurried out of the office, throwing me one last shy look. When she disappeared into the hallway, Michelle glanced up at me and hummed to herself, the way she always did when she had done something.

"Is she the reason you asked me to teach?" I asked.

"I thought you would like her," my sister said, setting the end of her pen on her lips and giggling softly. "I talked to her on the phone about a week ago, and she was a nervous wreck. She sounded so cute, and who would've known that she is?"

"Michelle ..." I twisted my head toward the window and watched Miss Monroe exit the club and head down the street toward the bus stop, her brown hair blowing in the breeze. "I can't teach this class."

My sister rolled her eyes. "You're so dramatic."

"I'm not dramatic," I argued. "I'm being reasonable."

"Unreasonable," Michelle said, smirking. "Because you won't do anything to her. You do remember what you told me last year after you sold your business, don't you? That you're done searching for a submissive. That you're going to be a grumpy old man by yourself."

"I didn't say that," I growled.

"Maybe not the last part, but you haven't been yourself since Mom died," she said.

"Mom dying has nothing to do with my life here."

She shrugged. "Well then, you should be fine teaching, huh? You don't want a submissive, and Sierra Monroe is *definitely not* your type. So, you don't have to worry about a thing! Right?"

I gritted my teeth and walked out of the room, heading straight for my office. After shutting the door behind me, I leaned against it and lifted my gaze to the window facing one of the many bus stops near our club.

Sierra bounced on her toes to keep warm, glancing back at the club. While she couldn't see me through the tinted windows, I couldn't pull my gaze away from her. I drew my tongue across my lower lip, dick twitching.

The way she couldn't stop blushing tonight, stuttering and stumbling over her words.

"Fuck," I growled.

This was going to be a long semester.

3

sierra

FUCK. I sprinted off the bus and down two streets while gazing at the time on my phone. *Thirty minutes late?! Why the hell did class get out so late?* I should've been here on time, like I had promised Steve —I meant, Professor Patton.

When I reached the entrance, I leaned over my knees to catch my breath and gazed up at the same security guards I had spoken with last night. "I-I'm here f-for class," I said between breaths, chest rising and falling.

"You're late."

"I know," I whispered. "Can I please come in so Professor Patton doesn't kill me?"

The stoic man chuckled and stepped to the side. I raced into the building without looking like a complete newbie in a room full of pro dominants and submissives, then found the back hallway, where the class was being held.

Still attempting to catch my breath, I pushed the door open and stepped into the room. All the seated students snapped their heads toward me while Professor Patton glanced up from the open textbook in his hand, his dark eyes on me.

"Sorry I'm late," I whispered, closing the door softly behind me.

From the door in the back of the room, I scanned the room for an empty seat.

Professor Patton snapped the book closed and tapped an empty desk, front and center. I gulped and hurried down the aisle of seats toward the front of the room, my gaze not leaving his smoldering one once.

Once I finally collapsed into the seat, I scrambled to set my belongings at my feet and pulled out a pen. All the other students had open textbooks, and I cursed myself for not coming sooner. I hated the attention.

"As I was saying, if you feel uncomfortable with anything during this class"—he looked solely at me, his dark gaze lingering, and tugged on his tie to loosen it—"your safeword this semester will be *unicorn*. Do you understand?"

Students in class nodded.

"I need a verbal response," he said.

In unison, students murmured in response.

He stepped toward me, his gaze making me feel all sorts of things that, as his student, I shouldn't feel at all. He cleared his throat, his large hand sprawling across the desk. "Miss Monroe?"

"I understand," I murmured.

"Louder."

My cheeks flushed from embarrassment. "I understand."

"Good girl."

Warmth exploded between my thighs, my nipples aching from two words. *Two freaking words*, and he already had me a wet, sopping mess. We weren't even alone, and he … he had no problem with calling me a … a good girl.

Fuck.

"This is a contract," he said, handing a stack of papers to each person in the front row.

I took a sheet from the stack and passed it back to the student behind me. Grabbing my pen, I glanced down at the sheet labeled *Sex Education Class Agreement*, along with an attached syllabus with classes named Throat Fucking 101, Obedience 101, Degradation 101, and … much more.

"You don't need a contract for every type of relationship that you find yourself in, but we'll be going through some basic BDSM in this class, so I'm required to introduce you to the contractual side of a sexual relationship."

The contractual side?

My gaze drifted down the page as I briefly scanned it. According to this, we'd get a textbook that explained different types of sexual intercourse and the basics of BDSM, like relationships and partnerships, toys, and more.

"If you continue down the page," he said, as if he had been talking and I had completely zoned out while staring at the glaring words of *dominance and submission, master and slave, sadist and masochist.*

"Will there be demonstrations?" someone asked to my left.

"Yes."

Snapping my gaze to him, I sucked in a sharp breath and pressed my thighs together.

Did he say demonstrations? *How is he going to demonstrate? What will he demonstrate? The sex positions? How to be a dom? On a student?*

On … me?

"Sierra, you'll learn how to properly masturbate during this class, so you won't have to grind those thighs together," he said, peering up from the master contract he held and smirking at me. "I doubt that makes you feel any good, does it?"

I sucked in another sharp breath, heat exploding through my core and cheeks reddening. I opened and shut my mouth three times in a row, attempting to find the words to respond. But everyone was staring at me, and I couldn't get anything out but, "Sorry, sir," as I stopped rubbing my legs together.

"I didn't say to stop," Professor Patton said, returning to his paper. "Continue."

Cheeks flaming hot, I dropped my gaze to the desk in front of me and tried to ignore all the other students' stares. *Why did he call me out like that?* I hadn't even realized that I had been so … uncomfortable.

My nipples poked against my shirt, and I pressed them against the desk so nobody could see them. My body felt like it was on fire, like the flames were overtaking every inch of my skin, my thighs, my pussy.

Fifteen minutes later, once I finally calmed down, Professor Patton walked behind his desk. "That's all for tonight. I'll see you all next week." He glanced up at me. "Sierra Monroe. Please, stay after. We need to chat."

So, as all the students cleared out of the room, I quietly gathered my belongings and hoped that everyone would completely forget that I even existed. I wanted to crawl into a hole and die after tonight.

Once I slung my backpack over my shoulder, I walked to the front.

He handed me a book. "Please read the first three chapters by the next class."

"What is this?"

"A book on sex. Chapters one through three detail consent as well as the basics."

"Okay," I whispered, holding it to my chest. "I'll read them by the next class."

"And," he said before I could leave, "we need to talk about your disobedience."

"My disobedience?"

"Your tardiness."

"One of my classes ran over," I said, nipples taut. "She usually lets us out five minutes early so I have time to catch the bus. But I had to"—I laughed nervously—"grab a later bus, then run here tonight. It won't happen again. I promise."

"We need to make sure of that, especially for the demonstrations." He shook his head. "But either way, I ordered you not to be late." He moved closer to me and lifted my chin. "And you disobeyed me."

"I-I didn't mean to," I whispered.

"Disobedience is punished in my class."

"Punished?" I repeated, pressing my thighs together. "H-how will you do that?"

His lips curled into a small smirk. "Follow me."

4

"WHERE ARE WE GOING?" Sierra whispered, gazing at the people inside the glass rooms as we walked through the Hall of Glass.

One room in particular that she couldn't seem to pull her eyes away from had a woman bent at the hip with men in each of her holes.

"This way," I hummed, amused.

Sierra sucked in a sharp breath and blushed, then continued with me down the hallway.

"For the first half of class, I became acquainted with other students' prior experience. Since you conveniently missed it, I need you to show me the extent of your sexual experiences," I said. "How far have you gone?"

"I, um … haven't done much."

I placed my hand on her lower back, restraining myself from dragging my hands all over her body, and guided her toward a private room in the back of Radiant, which was exclusively available only to owners.

A smirk tugged at my lips. "Oh, no, Sierra. I said that you're going to show me."

"Show you," she repeated, eyes wide. "H-how am I supposed to do …" She stopped in front of the glass room, gulped, and pointed to the door. "You want me to show you in … here? A-are people going to watch?"

Gently taking her chin in my hand, I drew my thumb across her lower lip. "Only me."

When her jaw lolled, I swiped my thumb across her lip again and watched her tongue travel across it, her eyes softening and her body relaxing more than it had all night. A perfect little submissive for me.

"Will you do that for me?" I asked.

"Yes," she whispered, pressing those thighs together again, "sir."

Fuck.

I pushed my thumb into her mouth and let her suck on it. "Good girl."

After another moment, I pulled my thumb from her mouth and led her into the room. She stepped in, pupils dilating at the various ropes and whips hanging from the wall. Her nipples hardened underneath her shirt, poking against the material.

When she finally took it all in, I hit a switch on the wall.

"What's that light switch for?" she asked, turning toward me, flustered.

"To make the glass dark so nobody can see into the room." I guided her toward the bed. "Why don't you relax?"

Once she sat down, her knees jittery, she glanced at me. "This is wrong," she whispered.

"If you're not comfortable, you have a safeword," I reminded her. "Remember?"

"Yes," she said in a breath.

"What is it?"

"*Unicorn.*"

"If you want to stop, you will use it. Understand?"

"Yes."

I waited for her to speak the word back to me, waited for her to tell me that she didn't want this, that I was overstepping, that she was never returning to my class ever again. But she lay back on the bed.

"Y-you said that you wanted me to show you what I've done?" she asked.

"It's only fair that I know your experience before teaching you," I murmured.

"I only really have experience with … touching myself," she whispered, staring into my eyes but dipping her hand into her panties underneath her skirt. It fell open enough for me to see how ruined her panties were. She must've been this wet all night.

Unable to stop myself, I walked toward the bed and knelt on it with my knee. "Sierra …" I said in a weak attempt to control myself. She was so innocent, so shy, and still a fucking virgin. This was wrong of me. "Is this what you usually do?"

She glanced up at me through her dark lashes. "I-I'm not too good at it."

Crawling onto the bed, I moved closer to her as her legs seemed to fall apart on the bed for me. I swallowed hard, gazing down from her lips to her taut nipples to that pussy glistening through her underwear.

I should have stopped, but I wanted to drag my mouth all over her.

"Sorry it's taking a long time," she whispered. "I'm bad at this."

"Is that what he told you?"

"Wh-what?"

"Is that what your ex-boyfriend told you?" I asked because she hadn't stopped repeating that all night. I moved closer to her, wanting to touch that drooling little cunt for her and show her that it was *him* who hadn't known how to touch her, how to make her feel good. "Hmm?"

She stared down at me and rubbed her pussy faster, gaze dropping to my fingers that lingered dangerously close to her cunt.

Closer than they should've. She was my new student, almost half my age.

"Answer me, Miss Monroe," I ordered. "Is that what your ex-boyfriend told you?"

"Yes," she whispered, pulling her hand away. "I'm sorry. I—"

"Don't stop," I growled. "You're going to rub that little pussy for me until you come. I don't care how long it takes, how long I have to lie here and watch your cunt quiver for me. I'll stay here all night if I have to."

After she sucked in a sharp breath, she placed her hand back, her body jerking slightly.

"There it is," I murmured. "Just like that."

She rubbed her clit faster in small circles. "I-I usually … use toys and watch …"

"Watch?" I asked, brow arched and a smirk tugging at my lips.

"P-porn."

A small chuckle escaped my mouth. "What kind?"

Cheeks tinting red, she turned her head to the side and buried her face into the pillow. But I took her chin in my hand and forced her to look back down at me. She wasn't going to get out of this one.

"What kind?"

She averted her gaze. "A bit of everything."

"Everything?"

"Yes," she said in a small voice.

"Eyes on me, Miss Monroe," I ordered.

She peered at me.

"You watch everything?"

"Maybe not everything," she whispered, as if she was too embarrassed to speak about the type of porn she watched aloud, but she had been the one to bring it up, the one who had initially wanted to speak about it.

And I could see her pussy tightening.

"What do you watch?"

"Well, this week, I've watched some …" She furrowed her brow, stared down at me, and rubbed her pussy harder, her full lips forming a small O and pleasure rushing over her expression. "Some BDSM stuff."

Fuck. If she keeps this up …

"What kind?"

"Um …" She looked away for a brief moment, then snapped her gaze back to me as if she remembered that I'd ordered her to keep her eyes on me. "I watched some light … dominant and submissive scenes." She sucked in a breath, her body tensing. "With rope."

"Bondage?" My lips curled into a smirk. "Does that excite you, Sierra?"

She nodded.

"We'll have a class on that," I hummed, wanting nothing more than to tie her up right here and right now. I hadn't touched a rope in nearly a year now, but my fingers ached to glide against the coarse edges.

My gaze dropped to her drooling pussy as I ground my dick against the mattress as discreetly as possible. This was wrong. She was my student, who trusted me to show her the ropes—quite literally.

"You're doing great," I praised. "That little pussy is quivering already."

Legs beginning to tremble, she whimpered, "Professor Paaaatton."

I drew my tongue across my lower lip, wanting nothing more than to dip my head and place my mouth all over her cunt. I wanted to feel her crying out all over my face, my tongue on her clit, tasting her pleasure.

"You can go faster, can't you, love?" I breathed heavily. "For me."

She rubbed her pussy faster, back arching and legs shaking.

"Just like that," I whispered, grinding my cock into the mattress. "Let me hear you."

After she flicked her fingers over her clit once more, her shoulders lifted off the mattress as she cried out louder than I'd expected.

Her little pussy pulsed over and over, desperate for me to be inside it, filling it.

And I could only imagine how fucking sexy she'd look with my cum dripping out of her.

When she finally relaxed against the mattress, I gathered myself and shuffled off the bed before she could see the raging boner that I had stuffed inside my pants. I cleared my throat and stepped toward the door.

"A driver will pick you up from your class next week."

"A driver?" she repeated, shaking her head. "No, that's too much. I don't need someone to drive me back and forth between campus and here. I can walk if I miss the bus. It's honestly not too much, Professor Patton."

"He'll be there at eight thirty sharp," I said. "You're not missing my class again, Sierra."

Not for the first demonstration of the semester.

5

sierra

COCK RIDING 101.

On Monday night, I stared at the words written on the board with white chalk and swallowed hard. Professor Patton stood up front near his desk, chatting with a couple of students. I pressed my thighs together, unable to forget about what had happened after the last class.

He had been close to touching me. So close. And I had almost let him.

What was wrong with me? He was my Sex Education professor, for fuck's sake, twice my age, and an experienced member of Radiant. But he had ordered a driver to pick me up for class tonight, and he had followed me right into that glass room last Monday. That had to mean something, right?

I shook my head and walked to the empty desk up front and center. I was doing what I always did with men, looking for *anything* that could be taken as desire for me, looking for reasons why he'd want to take care of me.

When the girls who chatted with him sat down in their seats, Professor Patton finally turned toward the class, his gaze landing on me. Heat rushed through my body, and I whimpered softly to myself.

"I've split this specific class between enrolled females and males, so you girls would feel more comfortable for the first demonstration. Upcoming demonstrations will include both female and male students. Now, I asked you to bring a partner that you're familiar with for tonight," he said, strumming his fingers on the table. "Ah, Miss Monroe, I must've forgotten to mention it to you, seeing as you were late."

Partner?

After gazing around the room and realizing that I didn't recognize any of the males from last class—only the females—I glanced down at my desk and wondered what the hell I was going to do. *Will he fail me for not bringing a partner? Punish me?*

I drew my tongue across my dry lips, desperately trying to wet them, and thought about all the possibilities of what that punishment would look like. He'd seemed almost excited when I mentioned ropes and bondage the other night.

He cleared his throat, capturing my attention, then patted his knee. "Then, I'll be your partner for the night. You can start off the class by demonstrating what you learned in the first few chapters of your textbook *on me.*"

Everyone in the class turned in my direction, their heated gazes focusing in on me.

I stared at him through wide eyes and shook my head, my cheeks flushing even hotter. "I … I can't do that, Professor Patton. I …"

"It's demonstration day," he announced. "The majority of your grade is participation in these classes, and you don't have a partner. Do you want to fail and have to retake my course, Miss Monroe?"

I gulped and rubbed my thighs together, the heat raging in my core. "No, sir."

He patted his thigh again. "Then, come here and show me what you learned."

"O-okay."

Once I slid out of my seat, I nearly stumbled over my own two feet as I made it to his desk, my nipples hard and aching through the front of my shirt.

"What do you want me to do?" I whispered, shifting from foot to foot nervously.

"Ride my cock."

After inhaling sharply, I ground my thighs together and shuffled over to him. Throwing one leg over his, I straddled his waist and set my hands on his shoulders, my panties right against his bulge.

Oh my God. I can't believe I'm doing this.

"No, Miss Monroe," he said. "Without your clothes."

"Without my clothes," I breathed, eyes wide.

His gaze was dark, sinister, and dripping with lust. "Take them off, Sierra," he said, voice barely above a whisper. He glanced down at my nipples sticking out against the front of my shirt. "Every. Last. Piece. I want you naked."

As everyone watched me like this was the most normal thing ever, I stepped off him and crossed my arms nervously. This hadn't been in the syllabus. I mean, not that I remembered reading. But I had been so nervous in the first class.

He cleared his throat. "Why doesn't everyone start their demonstration, hmm?"

The females in the class pulled off their panties, lifted their skirts, and climbed onto their significant others, positioning themselves above their cocks and slowly sliding down onto them.

Like it was normal!

What is happening?!

Moans drifted throughout the class. My pussy tightened at the sounds and sights of each woman riding cock, their partner's hands all over their body. It wasn't like anything I'd ever seen before, the girls getting off on watching their friends get fucked.

"Miss Monroe," Professor Patton said, his gaze on nobody, except me. "Your turn."

After cursing under my breath, I pulled down my panties and skirt, then slowly pulled my shirt over my body, standing naked in front of him. He moved his hungry gaze down my body, his dick hardening inside his pants.

I pressed my thighs together, feeling the wetness pooling between them, and swallowed hard.

He lifted his gaze back up to me and patted his thigh once more. "Why don't you pull off my pants and straddle my waist?"

Once I took a deep breath, I dropped to my knees in front of him, wrapped my fingers around his waistband, and stared up at him. From over his pants, I could feel just how huge his cock really was. Luke's cock was nothing compared to his.

Professor Patton would tear my tight pussy apart.

Finally gathering up enough courage, I pulled down his pants and let his long, thick cock spring out of them. I whimpered at the sight, my sopping pussy clenching at the thought of him being deep inside me.

"Now, show me how good of a student you've been, Sierra." He sat back in the seat, slipped his hands underneath my armpits, and lifted me up to sit me on his lap. "Ride my cock until you milk out the cum from my balls."

He poked at my entrance and placed his large hands on my bare waist, sending shivers down my spine. I placed my hands on his shoulders again and moved my hips back and forth over the head of his cock, getting it wet with my juices.

"Are you sure this is okay?" I whispered.

I had never gone this far with anyone before, but I wasn't thinking clearly.

Maybe I was … imagining this all.

"Oh, Sierra," he grunted. "I've been waiting for this day since the moment you walked into Radiant. It wouldn't have mattered if you had brought your ex-boyfriend today or not. I still would've slid myself into you and come inside your tight hole."

Instead of waiting for me, he slammed my hips down on his cock and filled me up. I curled my fingers into his shoulders and gasped, the pressure rising high in my core. My pussy tightened around his shaft, legs trembling with pleasure.

God, he felt good. Too good.

He slid his hands down to my ass and cupped it. "Now, ride me."

I swallowed hard, already feeling the pressure building higher and higher in my core. Slowly, I bucked my hips back and forth on his cock, letting his dick slide out of my drooling pussy. I could feel every inch of him gliding against the ridges of my pussy.

"Faster," he commanded.

Bucking my hips faster, I slowly let my nerves go and pressed my breasts against his chest, staring down into his dark eyes and gripping his hair with one of my hands. My pussy tightened around him, the heat rising.

"Good girl," he murmured on my neck, staring up at me and moving my hips. "Keep tightening your pussy on my cock, just like you learned. Squeeze every last inch. Use your pussy to milk out my cum and make yourself feel good."

Whimpering, I moved faster and tightened myself even harder around him. I was close, so close to releasing around him. But I wanted to come at the same time that he did. I'd read that it felt best for both partners if they came at the same time.

"Please," I whispered. "I'm so close to coming. Please, come with me."

"You want my cum dripping out of your pussy?" he grunted against me. "Hmm?"

"Yes, Professor Patton," I screamed, throwing my head back. "Please, come inside my tight pussy!"

Hips bucking, I felt him grip my waist harder. I threw my head back and came all over his throbbing cock, knowing that my pussy was milking out every last drop of cum, knowing that my professor was giving me *all* of him.

Knowing that I had only known him for less than a week and he had taken my virginity.

6

steven

WITH MY CUM spilling out of her, Sierra slipped off me and stumbled back into the desk. I stared hazily at her dark brown hair cascading down her shoulders, my dick softening but my balls warm and heavy once more.

I wanted to fill her little hole again. And again. And again.

Make her take every last drop of it until she couldn't hold it inside of her any longer. Plug her holes up so she would be forced to feel my cum pool in her cunt, against her cervix. Breed her like the dirty slut she was.

After biting back another grunt, I drew my tongue across my lower lip. This wasn't even supposed to happen. She was my student. But after the other night, when she had played with her pretty little pussy for me, I couldn't control myself. I had been thinking about her nonstop.

"You're welcome to leave," I forced myself to say to her and the class before I pulled her onto me again. I stood, stuffed myself back into my pants, and zippered them, my breath quickening from the thought, the need to come inside her again making my dick swell.

In the past forty-four years of my life and the past twenty

running this club, that thought—*that kink*—had never crossed my mind, had never excited me. Until now. Until Sierra Monroe had wandered into Radiant.

From the corner of my eye, I watched Sierra pick up her clothes from the floor, tug them on, and then smooth them out. She tucked some hair behind her ear, cheeks flushing, and grabbed her belongings.

And while I wished she'd leave with the rest of the students so I could gather myself, she lingered behind until every last one of them left the room. When the door shut softly behind the last woman and her boyfriend, Sierra cleared her throat.

"Um, I …" she whispered.

I lifted my gaze. "Louder, Miss Monroe."

"I wanted to thank you for finding me a ride tonight," she said.

"Couldn't have you miss our first demonstration."

"No," she said, playing with the ends of her skirt.

My gaze dropped to her bare legs, and I spotted my cum on her inner thigh. I raised my fist to my mouth and bit down on my knuckle, dick twitching inside my pants. I'd bet her panties were soaked in my cum.

"Come here," I said softly after calming myself down.

She widened her eyes, her brow slightly furrowed. "Huh?"

"Come here."

When she finally padded over to me, I pulled off my loosened tie and wiped my cum off her inner thigh. She tensed and inhaled at the touch, watching me carefully and furrowing her brow even more.

"What are you doing?" she whispered.

"Cleaning you up."

"Why?"

"Because aftercare."

"Aftercare?" she repeated.

"Did you not read the chapters that I'd assigned you? There was a section on after—"

"I read it," she said in a breath. "But I didn't think it meant after

…" She sucked on her inner cheek and teetered from foot to foot, her gaze dropping. "I mean, we are just in a Sex Education class. I thought it was …"

"For committed relationships?" I finished. "No."

"Oh," she murmured.

"Do you need fresh clothes? Underwear?"

Cheeks red, she nodded. "If you have any, that would be nice. I have a long ride home."

I held out my hand for her to place her panties in. She stared at it for a moment, then placed her books on the desk and shuffled out of her underwear. She glanced at the trash, as if she was going to disobey me and toss them out, then she placed them into my hand.

"Good girl," I cooed, earning another blush.

"Professor Patton," she whispered, following me out of the classroom and into the main hallway toward the closet, where Michelle made sure to keep fresh clothes in case there was any type of accident. "Was what we did … okay?"

After handing her some fresh underwear, I turned around to face her, looking for any sort of regret on her face. "Why are you asking? You do remember your safeword, don't you, Miss Monroe? If you didn't—"

"It's not that I didn't want it—or even like it," she added, face turning a darker shade. She played with the ends of her skirt again, avoiding eye contact with me. "But you're my professor and so much older and more experienced than I am."

"You don't have to participate," I said honestly to her. "Stop me at any time if you don't feel comfortable because I am a greedy bastard and will take and take and take whatever I want—that is, until you speak your safeword."

"O-okay—"

"How was your first real class?" Michelle asked, walking into the hallway toward us with a stack of papers and beaming at Sierra.

"Good." Sierra tucked some hair behind her ear. "I need to head home."

"Not so fast," I said, catching her arm before she could escape. "You're not walking."

"The next bus is in forty-five minutes," she said. "I have to—"

Once I waved good night to Michelle, I pulled out a set of keys from my pants pocket and placed my hand on her lower back, guiding her from the front of the club to a side door, which was for exclusive use.

She glanced up at me and shook her head, as if she wanted to argue with me. But I would have none of it. I wouldn't let any student walk home this late at night.

After unlocking my car, I opened the door for her. She stared at it through wide eyes for a moment, mouth dropping open slightly. My dick twitched as the thought of pushing myself between those full lips drifted through my mind.

"This is your car?" she asked, sitting in the passenger seat. "It's so nice."

"Yes," I said, shutting the door softly behind her, then slipping into the driver's seat.

I set my buzzing phone on the center console, ignored the call from my financial adviser, and started the car. Last year, I had sold the artificial intelligence software company that I had been building since eighteen and invested the majority of the money back into stock and properties for low-income and financially struggling families. And Jeff, my adviser, sometimes didn't know when to *stop* calling me about potential opportunities.

I respected it, but I had enough on my plate right now.

Like figuring out how not to … think about Sierra the way that I was.

———

Fifteen minutes later, after following Sierra's directions to Forbes Avenue in Oakland, I pulled up to the side of an apartment building right on the main street. A group of rowdy college-aged guys sat outside on the curb, hiding beers.

"You live here?" I asked.

"Yeah," she said, glancing out the window. "With a roommate."

When she pulled on the handle, I grabbed her wrist. "You're safe here?"

She giggled nervously. "As far as I know."

I released her wrist and let her exit the car, swinging her backpack over her shoulder.

"See you next week, Professor Patton," she said, glancing in through the window.

"I'd actually like you to attend Thursday's class, Miss Monroe," I said, unable to stop myself.

She had no reason to be at Thursday's class with the guys, but like I had told her, I was a greedy bastard who would take what she gave me.

"With the guys?" She widened her eyes. "You would?"

I tightened my hand around the steering wheel. "Yes, I would. And you might want to bring a spare change of underwear for it. You're going to need them."

7

sierra

"SO," Heather hummed once I walked out of class, "tell me all about it!"

She usually waited for me every night outside the Cathedral of Learning—or Cathy, as we called it—so we could walk back to the apartment that her parents, thankfully, paid for. I was so grateful for them, especially after what had happened with my family a few years back.

"Tell you about what?" I asked, clutching my books to my chest and blushing.

Yesterday, I might've sorta told her that I was attending a Sex Education class with a very handsome professor. I'd promised I'd save all the juicy details for our walk home today, but I hadn't expected to actually lose my virginity to him!

"Don't play, Sierra. You know what I'm talking about. Your Sex Ed course!" She nudged me and stopped at the outdoor Crazy Coffee Bar to grab a drink for the walk. "Wasn't your second class, like, cock riding or something like that?"

"Yes," I whispered, glancing around at the students looking at us. "Can you quiet down?"

After I gave my order to the cashier, we waited in the cold for our orders while other students lingered around with their friends. I bounced on my toes, my cheeks red from the windchill and from thinking about last night.

I had lost my virginity!

I still couldn't believe it.

Once most of the students grabbed their orders and headed to their dorms, Heather beamed next to me. "So, tell me about it. Did you learn how to ride dick?" She wiggled her eyebrows. "So you can stop humping your pill—"

"I do not do that!" I scolded quietly. "You're one to talk. You're a virgin too."

She smirked. "Not for long."

My eyes widened. "What do you mean?"

"I mean that I've been chatting up this guy online," she said, smirking. "I met him on a BDSM website."

I slapped her shoulder. "Heather! Why didn't you tell me?!"

"Because it hasn't happened yet, but something has with you," she gushed. "You've literally been glowing since this morning. And I might've been peering out the window when that nice car dropped you off the other night. So, what happened?"

Biting back a smile, I leaned forward. "We had some demonstrations."

"Shut up."

"I'm being serious, Feather," I hummed, using her nickname. "And they were ... *very explicit.*"

With her pupils dilated, she grasped my hand. "Like real-life demonstrations?! Were there people who actually came in and fucked in front of the class?! How do I sign up because I need to—"

"Quiet down," I said in a hushed tone again. "And no. Not other people."

She furrowed her brow. "Then, how were there—oh shit!" She slapped my arm repeatedly and jumped up and down, causing a whole scene in the middle of campus. "Bitch, don't tell me you lost your virgini—"

I smacked a hand over her big mouth and yanked her behind the coffee shack building so nobody would be able to see us speaking about the dom who had taken my virginity at his BDSM club last night. Fuck, the more I thought that, the less it even seemed real.

Before I pulled my hand off her mouth, I arched a brow. "Will you please keep it down?"

While she nodded, I hesitated even pulling my hand away. But eventually, I did and hoped that other students in my class didn't overhear. What would they think? I was twenty-three years old and had *just* lost my virginity to someone almost twice my age. Maybe older.

"Tell me all about him," she cheered. "Is he another student?"

"No."

"What do you m—bitch!"

My cheeks burned with embarrassment. Oh my God.

"It was your professor, wasn't it?!" she asked, literally almost jumping up and down at my side. She grasped on to my hand, shaking it, because she couldn't even control herself. How would she react once she finally lost her V-card?!

"Feather, will you—"

She placed the back of her hand on her forehead and closed her eyes. "Give me a second, Sea, before I pass out. My vagina is so wet, thinking about you getting it on with an elderly—"

Although she was causing a scene, I couldn't stop myself from bursting out into a fit of giggles. "He is not elderly! He is probably, maybe in his mid-forties. And I mean, he's one of the handsomest men I have met."

"Oh, girl," Heather said, fanning herself. "I bet he is. Do you have a picture?"

"Who do you think I am?" I asked. "Some sort of creep?"

"Maybe."

"Pictures are forbidden in the class," I said. "So, no."

She frowned. "Can't you sneak one?"

"And get punished for it?!" I exclaimed, but then I stopped and thought about it for a minute because I would bet that a punishment from Professor Patton wouldn't be so bad. Then, I shook my head. "No. No, I can't."

"Lame."

"Heather! Sierra!" the cashier called from the other side of the small building.

Heather looped her arm around mine and tugged me to get our coffees. I grabbed the warm drink, sipped in an attempt to rid myself of the cold, and locked eyes with Luke Carls, my *lovely* ex-boyfriend who had ditched me two weeks ago.

He leaned against the building next to the window and smirked. "Sierra Monroe."

Mid-sip, I froze. "What are you doing here?"

After kicking himself off the building, he lifted his coffee cup. "Coffee."

"You don't drink coffee."

"And you're not usually easy," he said, sipping his drink and walking over to Heather and me. Heather tugged me closer to her. "At least when we were together, you weren't. But things change, don't they?"

"Why don't you leave?" Heather asked.

"I'm not easy," I said.

"So, you didn't just gift your *precious little virginity* to your professor?" he asked with a smirk. "I might've overheard you gushing to Heather, hiding behind the building, about how much of a cheap whore you've become in the past two weeks."

I crossed my arms and ignored him. Or at least, I *tried* to.

"Ignore him," Heather said, pulling me along with our coffees.

"Miss Monroe!" someone called from across the street.

"Who's that?" Heather said.

I followed her gaze and locked eyes with Leo, my driver to Radiant from the other night. Shit, Professor Patton had requested that I attend the guys' class tonight, and I had completely forgotten!

"Oh, um," I said, leaping up and gathering my stuff, "a driver for me."

"A driver?!" Heather gushed. "What is this guy, a billionaire or something?"

Luke scowled. "Like she'd ever be able to score a billionaire."

"Nobody's talking to you," Heather growled. "Leave us alone."

I pulled Heather far away from him, then grabbed her hand. "I have sorta, kinda been requested to attend another class this week. Professor Patton wanted to … see me again for some reason."

"Because you have an amazing pussy."

After smacking her hard, I looped my hands around my backpack straps and hurried across the street. "I'll see you later tonight! Don't wait up for me!"

8

sierra

"MISS MONROE IS a student from my other course," Professor Patton announced to his male students in his class, Fucking 101. He placed a hand on my shoulder and squeezed. "She wanted some extra credit for the semester and offered to participate in today's demonstration class."

I sucked in a sharp breath and stared up at him. I had offered no such thing, but I wasn't going to argue with him. Not after I had come by just bouncing over and over on his huge, fat cock.

"Isn't that right, Sierra?"

"Yes, sir," I said, staring at the hungry male students.

"Each of you will take turns demonstrating what you learned in your first reading," he announced to the class. "You're all going to fuck Miss Monroe until you make her come all over your cock, and then you're going to fill her pussy. Understand?"

A wave of grunts and nods filled the room. Professor Patton turned toward me.

"Miss Monroe," he said, patting his desk, "remove your clothes to get these boys hard, then sit on the edge of my desk and spread your legs. We all want to see that glistening little pussy you have."

Heat gathered between my legs. I shifted from foot to foot in front of the classroom full of men and slowly started stripping my clothes. When I stood in just my bra and soaked panties, I swallowed hard and reached behind myself to unclip my bra. It fell to the ground at my feet, my tits bouncing out of it.

A couple of grunts drifted from the group of guys. I shimmied out of my panties and slid onto the desk, peeking over at Professor Patton, who stood at the side of the class and crossed his large arms over his chest, smirking in approval.

"Spread your legs."

After placing my hands behind me on the desk, I spread my legs and let the guys stare at my pussy, which couldn't stop clenching. Murmurs and grunts erupted throughout the room. I ached to pull my legs together to feel some friction between them, but I held myself back.

"First student," Professor Patton announced. "Why don't you step up to the front of the class and show me what you learned?"

One guy from the back of the class walked up to me and undid his pants, sliding them down to his knees and whipping out his huge cock. He rubbed his head against my clit, back and forth and back and forth, pushing me higher.

I whimpered softly, throwing my head back. "Please."

He positioned himself at my entrance and slid into me. Once every inch of him was inside me, he gripped my waist and pulled me toward him with every single thrust. I curled my toes, still holding my legs as far apart as they would go.

Pressure rose in my core, and I moaned, "More! Please, more!"

Trailing one hand down to my clit, he spit on it and rubbed the spit over and over across the sensitive bud, sending a wave of pleasure through my body. My body jerked up into the air, an orgasm ripping through me. My legs trembled as I screamed out in pleasure.

He pumped into me for two more thrusts, then stilled deep inside my pussy. When he finally came inside me, he thrust his cum even deeper, then pulled out of me. I pulled my thighs together when he stepped away and pulled up his pants.

"Spread. Your. Legs." Professor Patton clenched his jaw from the side of the room, giving me those dark eyes. "You have more men to please today, Sierra."

So, I spread my trembling legs even further apart and readied myself for the next guy, who stepped up and positioned himself at my entrance. He slammed himself inside me harder and rougher, grabbing my throat in one hand and smacking my tits over and over in the other until they became red.

I cried out, the pressure already building higher. "Give it to me!" I screamed, letting him use my hole for his pleasure.

He strummed his fingers across my fragile throat and stuck his thumb into my mouth, forcing me to suck it. I stared into his eyes, tightening my pussy around his huge cock, and whimpered on his finger, "Please."

Grunting, he stilled deep inside me. I cried out and came at the same time, unable to hold it back.

Before I knew it, a line formed behind him, each guy readying himself to fuck me senseless and fill me with his cum. And after every last guy filled me to the brim, their cum was spilling onto the desk and dripping onto the tiled floor.

There was so much of it inside me that I couldn't even hold it in, like Professor Patton had instructed in my Cock Riding class. I tried to hold it in as best as I could, but it continued to drip out of my pulsing pussy.

Professor Patton walked over to me and captured the cum on his fingers, then shoved them into my mouth. "Didn't I tell you not to waste any cum?" he asked, forcing me to lick all the cum off my fingers. "I know your pussy is tight, Sierra, but if you can't hold it all in, then you must swallow it."

I moaned on his fingers and nodded, legs still spread and desperate for him to fuck me too. I didn't know what had happened to me, but whatever he had done to me, it had worked.

I craved every single part of him.

When he pulled his fingers out of me, he glanced down at my drooling pussy. "If you want me to fuck you, then make room in that pretty little pussy of yours because I'm not letting you take my cum anywhere other than your cunt."

Shoving my fingers into my pussy, I coated them with their cum and then stuck them into my mouth, hungrily sucking off the juices, desperate for him to come inside me too. I rubbed the excessive cum into my clit and spread my legs.

"Please, sir," I whimpered, "put it inside me."

He smirked and undid his pants, then shoved his huge cock into my pussy to please me. I screamed out in pleasure as he thrust in and out of my hole, faster and harder than any of the guys had, showing them what it really meant to fuck a woman.

"More, Professor!" I threw my head back and moved my hips with his. "More!"

He roughly sucked on my neck and picked me up off the desk. I wrapped my legs around his waist and let him bounce me up and down on his cock, getting deeper and deeper each time. He was getting deeper than any of the others, almost hitting my cervix, and I knew that at any moment, he would …

He grunted into my ear and stilled.

He came right against it, giving me every single last drop of his cum.

9

steven

ONCE I RELUCTANTLY PULLED OUT OF Sierra, I pressed my thumb against her clit and shivered in pleasure when it quivered underneath it. One last time, her shoulders jerked forward, and she cried out loud, ecstasy crossing her face.

"Good job," I murmured, doubting that she could even hear me.

She was lost in her own little world, and I fucking loved every moment of it.

"You are all free to leave," I said to the group of guys, clearing my throat and readjusting myself.

They filed out of the class in an unorganized line, hair tousled and clothes barely put back on correctly.

I shut and locked the door behind the very last one, then turned back to Sierra.

"You did amazing today, Sierra," I praised softly.

On my desk, she leaned back onto her hands and stared hazily at the closed door. I readjusted myself and stepped toward her.

"How do you feel?"

"Like a dirty whore," she said with the straightest face. And then she giggled. "I loved it."

I released a breath and thanked God that she hadn't gone through all that without using her safeword if she really didn't want to do it. By the looks of it, she had enjoyed it, but I needed to make sure. It was important to me.

After grabbing a towel from one of the closets, I wiped off the cum and wetness from her thighs and around her pussy lips, then pulled her skirt up her legs to cover her. She watched my every move, even when I walked to the trash and dumped the towel.

"Why do you do that?" she asked.

"Do what?"

"Clean me up when we're finished."

"Aftercare," I said. "I thought we talked about this."

"We did, but I just … can't believe it," she whispered to herself.

"It's my job to make sure you're okay."

"Yeah, but … nobody has done something so nice for me before," she whispered.

My chest tightened, and a frown tugged at the corner of my mouth. I parted my lips to respond, but I couldn't come up with anything that didn't sound so forced. No *I doubt that's true* or *someone surely has.*

Truth was that I had stopped searching for a submissive for so long because I felt the same way. Nobody that I was interested in cared about me, about my past, about my needs. All they cared about was themselves.

Especially my birth parents.

She laid her hands in her lap and smiled softly at me. "Thank you again."

I placed my hand on her knee and gently squeezed. "You don't need to thank me."

Sierra lifted her hand a couple of inches off her lap, paused for a moment, as if she was reassessing our current position, then swiped some hair off my forehead. I closed my eyes, enjoying the fluttery touch of her soft fingers.

A moment of easy silence passed between us, and then I finally gathered hold of myself, grasped her hand, and helped her off the desk. She winced slightly, taking her time sliding off the wooden table.

"Are you sore?"

She blushed. "A bit in the nether regions."

"Do you have a bath at home?" I asked.

"A bath in my apartment?" She laughed softly. "No."

I paused, wondering if what I wanted to say next would be crossing a line. After all, she was still my student. She trusted me to teach her the ropes, and she wasn't my submissive. Not yet. But I had crossed many lines already, from the moment I had stayed in Michelle's office while she signed up for my class.

"What is it?" she asked.

"Can I run a bath for you?" I finally asked.

She widened her eyes. "I, um … you don't have to. I'm sure I'll survive."

"I want to."

She opened and closed her mouth a few times. "Where's the bath?"

"I have a highrise about a block down the road," I said. "I'll bring you home right after."

"It's dangerous to go home alone with a man I just met," she said.

"Then, I'll grab a heating pad for you from the office and bring you home instead."

"No," she said, pulling her phone out of her backpack. "It's okay. Let me just text my friend your address, and we can go. But not for long. I have an internship and classes all day tomorrow."

———

"Th-this is your home?" she whispered, stopped in the middle of the foyer.

"One of them."

She gawked at the art on the walls and stepped farther into the skyrise, glancing around and giggling nervously as she pulled off her coat. "I don't want to break anything," she murmured. "It looks so expensive."

I took her coat and laid it on the couch for now, then guided her into the hallway and into the master bedroom to begin running the water. She slowly stripped off her clothes, wincing when she bent at the hip to peel off her skirt.

With bubbles in the bath and a wick candle burning on the counter, Sierra lay in my bath, naked. "Why'd you open Radiant?" she asked, leaning over the side, her arms glistening with water and bubbles in the candlelight.

She rested her head on her right shoulder and smiled softly. Though I could see some strain etched into her expression.

"Because I enjoy the atmosphere."

While her cheeks flushed, she urged, "But why?"

"Why?" I chuckled tensely. "Usually, that's enough of an answer."

"Not for me."

"Do you want an honest answer?"

She nodded.

"I like control, and I want to care for someone," I said, drawing my fingertips across the water. And I had wanted someone to care *about* me too, to trust me enough to lead them, to be able to lean on me whenever they needed.

"Is there a reason?" she asked.

A reason? For me being this way?

I tensed and gulped, unfamiliar nerves building inside my stomach. Usually, with women, I was in complete control. They never asked questions about my life, about my desires, wants, and needs. But now, I was lost for fucking words.

"You should ask this many questions during class, Sierra," I murmured.

"Sorry," she mumbled, sinking down in the bubbles with her cheeks tinting red. "I'm in grad school for psychology, and I like to understand people's motives. I've never been around anyone like you before. I find you interesting." She giggled softly. "In a good way."

"You don't have to apologize to me." I peered at her. "You do that a lot."

In a bath full of bubbles, she stared at the blank wall and frowned, her gaze distant.

"What's on your mind?" I asked.

"Do you think I'm easy?"

"Because of tonight? No, of course not."

"Not because of tonight," she whispered, sinking lower in the tub.

"Why are you asking? Where did this come from?"

She opened her mouth, then blew out a breath, bubbles forming where her mouth met the water. She closed her eyes and lolled her head against the back of the tub, sighing. "I don't know. Sorry I brought it—"

"Who told you that you were easy?" I growled.

Because this hadn't come out of nowhere. If this wasn't talking about tonight, then someone had put this thought—*those words*—into her head. And whoever the fuck it was, I would rip them a new one.

"Sierra," I said sternly, "who told you that you were easy? Someone at the club?"

"No," she whispered. "I ran into my ex today before class."

10

steven

MONDAY NIGHT, I stood outside the Cathedral of Learning's campus at eight twenty-five p.m., leaning against my Bentley with my arms crossed. Sierra should be relieved of classes in five minutes, and I wanted to be there when she was, so that stupid fucker ex-boyfriend of hers wouldn't harass her.

I tapped my fingers against my bicep and clenched my jaw, impatient.

After I had brought Sierra home the other night, I couldn't stop thinking about what she had told me, about how her ex had made her feel from a single one-sided conversation. I didn't know anything about the kid, except that he had hurt her. But that was enough.

My phone buzzed, and Leo's name flashed across the screen.

Leo: Are you sure?

Leo: I can pick up Sierra, Mr. Patton.

Instead of responding, I shoved the phone into my pocket and gritted my teeth. I had rescheduled all my meetings before class tonight so I could be here for her. Leo wasn't going to pick her up from campus anymore.

I would.

Two minutes after eight thirty, students began pouring out of the main door. I drew my tongue across my teeth and scanned the crowd for Sierra. And when the herd of students dwindled down to only a few, I rechecked Leo's text to make sure I was in the right place.

"God, he's so annoying," a young woman growled, tugging Sierra out of the building.

"I don't know why he's suddenly so interested," Sierra hummed.

"Because he's jealous," the other woman said. "Of you being with anyone else."

"Yeah, but—" Sierra lifted her gaze and stopped mid-sentence when she spotted me. Her cheeks turned bright red, and she turned toward her friend. "I have to go to, um, another class. I'll see you tonight."

The friend gazed at me, then turned to Sierra and smirked. They exchanged some quiet words, which only made Sierra giggle nervously. When someone stepped out of the door, following them, they both tensed. Then, Sierra walked away.

I fixed my gaze on the man behind Sierra's friend and narrowed my eyes, watching her walk away so he didn't follow her. If my assumptions were correct, that fucker was the boy bothering Sierra. But I couldn't see him in the cover of darkness.

"Professor Patton?" she said, cheeks flushing red. "What're you doing here?"

"I'm here to take you to class." *Where I'm going to shove my cock so deep inside you that you'll forget all about this insignificant scumbag lingering at the doorway, just waiting to follow you home.*

I gazed past her at the guy near the door. "Who's that?"

"Don't worry about him," Sierra said quickly, tugging on my arm.

"Is that your ex?" I asked, not budging.

"Professor," she started.

I grabbed her chin and lifted it so she looked me in the eye.

"Outside of the classroom, you will address me as Steven or Sir—do you understand?"

With wide eyes, she inhaled sharply.

"Do. You. Understand?" I asked. "Don't make me repeat it again, Sierra."

"Yes, Sir," she whispered.

My thumb found her bottom lip, and I dipped it into her mouth so that asshole would know that she was mine. That if he wanted to say anything to her, then he'd have to say it to me too. That he'd never attempt to hurt her again.

"Good girl," I praised. "Now, is that man glaring at us your ex?"

"Yes."

"That wasn't so hard, was it, love?" I asked.

"No," she whispered. "But what are you going to do to him?"

"Don't worry about that," I said, not pulling my gaze away from those tantalizing eyes once. I wanted her to know that tonight, tomorrow, and from here on out, she would be mine. All mine, for nobody to steal.

"But—"

"No," I said sternly.

She snapped her mouth closed, then nodded. "Okay."

I grabbed her hand and led her to the passenger side of my car, opening the door and allowing her to slip into the car. I followed and sat in the driver's seat, locking the doors, starting up the car, and gently grasping her chin once more.

"You're mine, Sierra Monroe," I said, gliding my thumb across her lower lip. "And you'll know that by the end of the night."

11

"I HOPE you don't mind getting messy today, Sierra," Professor Patton murmured.

I stared up at him from my desk, my core growing warm. After peering down at my desk, I shuffled my legs together, desperate to suppress the lingering ache between them. I didn't know what had happened, but I hadn't been able to stop thinking about him since the last class. He had split the last class by gender, but we were back to men and women being together.

"What's today's class, Professor?"

Professor Patton leaned against his desk, his biceps flexing against his baby-blue dress shirt. "Squirting 101."

My eyes grew wide. "Wh-what?"

He stepped toward me and placed his large hands on my desktop, leaning forward. "*You* are going to help me teach the class how to make a woman squirt," he repeated, as if I needed clarification.

"But I … I can't squirt. I have never done it before. It's impossible for me."

"Oh, Sierra," he said, cupping my chin and forcing me to gaze up into his dark eyes. "Nothing is impossible for you." He slowly drew his thumb across my lower lip. "I can make you do anything."

It sounded like a promise, like one day, I'd fall deep under his charm and do anything he wanted—not because I wanted a good grade in his class, but because I *needed* his cock, because I was mesmerized by it, *hypnotized* by him.

Once everyone joined class, Professor Patton looked at me and tapped his desk, as if he wanted me to hop up onto it so he could begin. I glanced around nervously—not that I should be anxious because these guys had been inside me on Thursday night—and scurried to the front of the class.

He placed a hand on my shoulder and squeezed. "Sierra has volunteered to help me in today's class, where you'll learn how to make a woman squirt." He sprawled his large hand across the desk and glanced at me. "Why don't you pull off your clothes and slide on up here?"

After gulping, I shimmied out of my skirt, panties, and tank top, then slid onto his desk. I hadn't squirted ever before and didn't even think it was possible for me. What if I … I couldn't and I ruined his entire demonstration?

"Lie back," he ordered.

Core warming, I did as he'd told me and lay back atop the papers spread across his desk. He crouched between my thighs, pulled my right leg over his left shoulder, and grabbed the back of my other leg in his hand.

"First," he announced to the class, "get her wet."

Without any further instruction, he dipped his head between my thighs and drew his tongue across my aching clit while looking up at me. I clenched and gripped the edges of the table, core pulsing already.

His stubble tickled my inner thighs as he flicked his tongue across my clit over and over again, making the bud even more sensitive to the touch. He gently placed my thigh onto his other shoulder and trailed his fingers down to my entrance, rubbing the wetness without pushing it inside me.

"Tease her pussy until you can see it pulse around nothing but air." He moved away from my aching pussy slightly to show the class how it clenched down on nothingness and stared up at me, lowering his voice. "So desperate for me to be inside you, aren't you?"

"Yes," I whispered.

When he slipped one finger into me, I clamped down on it and squeezed. I needed more of him, more of this. He knew exactly how to touch me to drive me closer to orgasm. He flicked his tongue across my clit again and inserted another finger.

As he stuffed me full with a third finger, he sucked my clit between his lips. I squirmed in his hold, pussy pulsing, and whimpered, the pressure rising quickly inside me. Like I usually did, I tightened my abdomen to build up to the orgasm faster, racing to that high.

"I know that you want to clench on my fingers and hold it all in," Professor Patton said. "But I need you to relax, Sierra. Relax your body, your mind, and this pretty little cunt of yours and come."

Slowly, I released my death grip on his wrist and stared up at the ceiling, my heart pounding inside my chest. I closed my eyes, breathed in deeply, then relaxed my pussy so it didn't squeeze his fingers off.

"Relax," Professor Patton whispered. "Even more. Empty that mind."

After relaxing the muscles in my face, I let out another deep breath and lay on his desk with my legs spread and his fingers deep yet unmoving inside me. He gently rubbed circles on my hip, letting me slip deeper into relaxation, allowing me to focus on one thing and one thing only.

His fingers.

He curled them against my G-spot, massaging the sensitive bundle of nerves.

"Stop clenching, Sierra," Professor Patton growled, sucking my clit between his lips. "And let fucking go all over me."

The pressure built so much higher than it ever had. My body tightening, I was afraid of the intensity inside my core. I clutched down on his fingers once more, about to burst. And when he finally flicked my clit with his tongue, I released all the tension inside me and—

My back arched hard. I screamed out in pleasure, my pussy pulsing around his fingers. Sensations that I'd never experienced before rushed through my body. Every touch, every breath, every flick was so much more intense.

"Once you make her squirt the first time," he announced to the class, massaging his fingers against my G-spot over again, not stopping until my pussy was crying all over him, "the next few times will be easy." He peered up at me with those dark eyes. "Isn't that right, Sierra?"

My legs trembled uncontrollably. I gripped on to the desk, curled my fingers around the edge, and cried out in pleasure as the ecstasy surged through my body. I opened my mouth, my words coming out completely incoherent.

Body numb. Mind empty.

"Miss Monroe," Professor Patton taunted, "when your professor asks you a question, you answer him." He continued to massage my G-spot with his two fingers as the hilt of his palm repeatedly smacked against my clit.

"I-I'm s-sorry," I stuttered, my head so foggy that I couldn't remember what he'd asked.

Professor Patton chuckled at me, pulled his fingers out of my cunt, and slapped my clit. My body jerked into the air, another orgasm ripping through me. I gripped on to the desk and screamed out in pleasure.

"Please," I begged, a desperate slut to be filled by him. "Fuck me, Professor."

As I lay flat on the desk, he wrapped his hand around the front of my throat. "I'll let you be my little fuckdoll later." He reached down to rub my clit in small, tortuous circles. "I have a class to teach."

After he smacked my clit again—making it more sensitive than ever—he nodded to one of the males in the class. The student approached me slowly, eyeing my salivating cunt and drawing his tongue across his lower lip.

When he brushed his fingers up my thigh, I whimpered and stared up at him. They traveled higher and higher up my body, millimeters from my pussy, and then he plunged them inside of my wetness until he was knuckle deep.

"How does he feel, Miss Monroe?" Professor Patton asked.

"Good," I whispered, arching my back. "So good."

But not as good as Steven. Nowhere even close.

The guy continued to pump his fingers into me as Professor Patton ordered me not to tense. I leaned back on the desk and gazed between my legs, pressure rising inside my core quickly because my professor was giving me those dark, dangerous eyes again.

Like he wanted to devour me tonight.

And, hell, I ached for him to.

Suddenly, pleasure surged throughout my body as an orgasm ripped through me. I gripped on to the desk and screamed out, body seizing, legs shaking, mind going absolutely blank again.

Another student came over and plunged his fingers into me, taking his turn to push me all the way to the very edge and tip me over it. I cried out in pleasure, heat coursing through my body and my nipples aching to be squeezed.

And then another student. And another.

When the fourth pushed into me, I glanced down between my legs and past the student's hand still plunged deep in my pussy. The papers on my professor's desk were drenched, ruined, completely doused by me. He chuckled softly, the sound making me clench.

"You've ruined all my papers," Professor Patton purred. "All that pleasure … you couldn't keep it in anymore, could you?"

When the pressure rose in my core again, I pulled my legs together. I couldn't have another orgasm like that again. It was way too much pleasure rushing through me. I couldn't even think straight.

"Hold your legs apart," Professor Patton ordered.

But I couldn't anymore. I could barely move without seizing, without the pressure rushing to my core. Everything was sore already, and we had barely made it through half the class who had to practice on me, forcing me to come over and over.

"Sierra," Patton said sternly.

"I-I can't!" I cried.

Instead of motioning for the next student to use my body, he stood up and walked over to me. I blew out a deep breath and relaxed against the desk, thankful that we were stopping because I didn't think I'd be able to handle another orgasm of *that* magnitude.

Professor Patton easily lifted me off the desk, leaned back on it himself, and maneuvered me so I sat in his arms helplessly, the backs of my knees in the crooks of his elbows, my back against his chest, and my swollen pussy hovering against his bulge.

"Next."

"Y-you're going to hold me?!" I exclaimed to Patton. "But I'll ruin your clothes."

This time, a female walked up to the front of the room and stuck her long fingers into my cunt, making my legs tremble. The pressure was too much, and I wanted to pull my legs together, but Professor Patton wouldn't let me move.

"Being drenched in your cum and being ruined are two different things, Miss Monroe."

Heat rushed to my core. I ground my hips against his bulge, needing him to be inside me, desperate to be filled, to unravel in his arms again and again and again. I never wanted to stop. I wanted his cock every moment of the day.

"B-but you can't do that! They'll be stained. You'll—"

"I'll what?" he purred into my ear. "Have to walk around with them on?" He chuckled menacingly. "Oh, Sierra, I don't think you get it. You're mine. I don't care who sees my pants stained with your cum."

As the words left his mouth, I came all over his student's fingers and screamed out in pleasure. Waves rushed through me, sending me over the edge, making me desperate. So desperate for Professor Patton.

When the next guy rammed his fingers into my hole, I bucked my hips back and forth against my professor's throbbing bulge.

"I know you want to fuck me," I pleaded with him. "So, do it. Please fuck me!"

He spread my legs even wider, hiking them up enough so he could seize my nipples with his fingers and tug on them. I screamed out, my mind buzzing, my entire body both numb yet raging with pleasure.

I didn't know if I could even recognize myself anymore.

I was begging for him. Pleading for his dick, for his fingers, for all of him.

Screaming. Crying. Coming.

Over and over.

"You don't get my cock until everyone makes you finish."

My chest heaved up and down. I needed to be filled—and not with fingers.

"Beg them to help you finish, and you'll get it sooner," Professor Patton said.

I stared at the three students who were left to help me squirt, who I needed to finger-fuck me until I came undone three more times. Three times, and I'd get Professor Patton's cock. Three times. Three.

My orgasms came and went faster with each one, and when everyone was finished, Professor Patton dismissed the class. Once all the students were gone, he gripped me tightly, growled low in my ear, and whipped out his huge, throbbing cock.

"Please, fuck me! Fuck me! Please! Please, I need—"

Before I could say another word, he rammed himself into me. "God, I've been waiting to be inside you all fucking day, Sierra. Your pussy's so warm and damn fucking tight," he grunted into my ear, pounding away inside me.

Barely able to move, I reached over my shoulder to grab him and did what I could to bounce on his huge cock. He grunted into my ear again, and I curled my toes. Pleasure coursed through my body, building higher than it had all night.

"More!" I cried out. "Please, I'm so close! Please, Professor. Please!"

When he tugged on my nipples harshly one last time, I threw my head back and screamed. My pussy pulsed around his huge cock, drenching it in my cum. He pounded back into me once more, then stilled deep in my pussy, his cum spilling inside me.

"Soon, I'm going to teach the class how to get a woman pregnant," he growled into my ear, slamming up into me one last time. "And you're going to take my cum in your pussy every night, be my willing example."

12

AFTER THE BATH fizzed with Foamy brand bubbles, I grabbed a loofah and dunked it underneath the water. Sierra pulled her legs to her chest and leaned forward, resting her head on her knees and humming softly.

I drew the loofah across her glistening bare back, my stress from managing the Radiant franchise, helping Michelle with her Plaything Co. sex toy brand, and finding suitable housing for low-income families today slowly dissipating.

Honestly, I didn't know where it had come from, but I had told her that I wanted to breed her tonight. And the thought wasn't leaving me alone. I wanted to shove so much of my cum into her tight little hole until she couldn't physically fit any more of it inside her. Until her belly was swollen and she was pregnant with my child, walking around my place.

"Do you like baths?" she said.

A quiet chuckle escaped my mouth. "I haven't been in a bath in years."

"Will you let me give you one?"

"What?"

She giggled and shrugged her shoulders. "You know, *aftercare*."

"That's not how it works," I said.

Even though that was *exactly* how it worked. Aftercare wasn't just about me taking care of her and her needs after a scene, but it also could—and should—work the opposite way too sometimes. Yet I hadn't been with anyone who asked about me.

Ever.

"Why not?" she murmured, leaning over the edge of the tub. "You have needs too."

"Maybe some other time."

She stuck out her pinkie. "Promise?"

"No."

Giggling softly, she grasped my wrist and wrapped her pinkie around mine to *force* me to give her a pinkie swear. Then, she sank back in the tub. "Too bad. You already pinkie-promised. No take-backs."

"I did no such thing." I chuckled.

"No, but seriously," she said, "will you let me? Please."

"Not tonight," I said nervously.

I didn't know *how* to respond because nobody had cared about me like that. Nobody had asked to take care of me even though that was what I so desperately wanted from a partner. Which was one of the many reasons I had given up searching for a sub who fit my tastes.

"But sometime?"

"Sure," I murmured, knowing that she would be gone by then. "Sometime."

Sometime had never come with the submissives that I had met. Sometime came for other doms, like Hector and Michelle. But never with me. Ever since childhood, I had been disappointed and left with empty promises.

Her stomach rumbled under the water.

"Is someone hungry?" I asked.

Cheeks reddening, she placed a hand underneath the water and over her stomach. "I usually have a snack right after class, but I didn't get much of a chance tonight. I'll have something once I get back."

When she stood up from the bath, the water and suds rolled down her body. I grabbed a towel from the closet and placed it around her shoulders to dry her off. Grasping the towel from me, she stepped out of the tub.

"Come with me," I said once she was dry. "Let's get you something to eat."

She followed me to the kitchen, and I opened the fridge.

"I'm not much of a cook," I admitted. "But I can have my chef make you something."

"You have a chef?" she asked.

"He lives on the floor below," I said, heading to my phone on the counter to call him.

"Don't be silly. It's almost midnight. I have snacks at home."

"You're hungry, Sierra. You're going to eat."

"No, I don't need a full meal. Really."

When she finally convinced me not to call Thornton, I opened the fridge and freezer to see if I had anything here that she'd want to eat. I rarely ate here anymore and spent most of my free time at Radiant or working on investing in startups.

"Oh my gosh!" she said, staring wide-eyed into the freezer. "You have so many boxes."

I peered over her shoulder at the three empty boxes of Swirl Scoops Ice Cream that I had been meaning to throw out. These had been Mom's favorites, and I had been sharing one with her—metaphorically—every night.

Scratching the back of my head, I pulled the empty boxes out of the freezer. "Yeah …"

"Are they that good?" she asked with a small smile.

"They're pretty good," I said.

She peered down into the freezer, spotting one last box. I folded the boxes and placed them in the recycle bin.

"If you'd like to, you can try one. There should be some left."

She pulled out the last box and gazed down into it. "No, it's fine."

I took it from her and handed her the last ice cream cup. "Take it."

"It's your last one," she said.

"I can buy more."

After her stomach growled again, she finally took it from me. "Are you su—"

"Sierra," I warned, wanting to feed her.

She was hungry and wanted one, and I was a shit cook.

"Fine," she said, tearing open the top and sinking her spoon down into it. She took a big bite of the ice cream, pupils dilating. Before she could get another word out, she sank her spoon back into the cup. "Where do you get these?"

"Giant Eagle."

Her eyes widened. "Giant Eagle Market District?"

"Yes. Why?"

"Which one? Shadyside or Robinson?"

"I think Thornton goes to Robinson."

Somehow, her pupils dilated even more. "That's my favorite place ever!"

"The grocery store?"

"Have you been?"

"No."

"No?!" she exclaimed. "We're going one day."

"It's a grocery store."

"No," she said, shaking her head for emphasis. "It's an experience."

My lips curled into a smile, and a low chuckle escaped my mouth. "An experience?"

"It's like the size of a football field with a huge selection of everything imaginable—a bar, hot food, a second floor where you can eat," she exclaimed, staring out the window and grinning. "I literally orgasm every time I walk into the store."

"I'd go just to see that."

She playfully smacked me. "You will love it."

13

sierra

WHEN WE PULLED up at my apartment building, three football players were lingering outside, bullshitting with each other. I didn't really *know*, know them, but they had always been nice to me, especially now that the season was ending.

Before I could exit his car, Steven grabbed my wrist. "You sure you're okay here?"

"I'll be fine," I said, pushing the car door open. "Really. I've lived here for a few months now, and nothing *particularly* bad has happened to our apartment yet. So, I don't think you should worry at all."

He arched his brow. "Particularly? Would you like to clarify?"

"Not really." I giggled nervously.

"What happened?"

"Nothing."

"Sierra."

"Steven," I murmured back, but then slapped a hand over my mouth.

Even he blinked in surprise.

While he had told me to call him by his first name outside of class, it still felt … weird. Foreign. Like I wasn't supposed to say it. He was my professor who taught Sex Education, for fuck's sake! Not my boyfriend.

"Okay," I said, wanting to get out of here before I said something *really* embarrassing. "Well, I gotta go. I have an early morning class tomorrow that I need to wake up for, and if I stay out here any longer …"

I might ask to go back home with him.

Once I forced myself to slam his car door, I hurried past the athletes, who gazed at Steven's car.

"Good night," I called over my shoulder as I jogged up the steps to the apartment building.

I tapped my student ID on the buzzer and slipped past the doors once it beeped. After I gave my ID to security, I stepped onto the elevator with butterflies in my stomach.

One day maybe soon, I would get to give Steven a bath. And while it wasn't a big deal for everyone, I hadn't given anyone a bath in years … after what had happened with my family. I missed being able to care for people.

Hopefully, when I asked him next time, he wouldn't freeze up, and he'd actually hop into the bathtub with me. My lips curled into a smile when I reached my floor, my stomach light. God, I really hoped so.

Only bad part was that I wouldn't see him for about a week.

A week!

"Bitch!" Heather squealed when I walked into the apartment. She was lying on the couch, smirking devilishly at me and pausing her laptop that was hooked up to the flat screen TV with an HDMI cable. "Another spicy night with the professor?"

I ran a hand over my face and giggled, closing my Foster Family textbook for my psychology grad program that I had left open on the counter. I grabbed it to finish my work in my bedroom for my internship tomorrow at Heron Adoption Agency.

"Well, your girl has a *date* on Friday night," she said from the living room.

"A date?" I asked. "With who?"

"He owns a sex club downtown."

My eyes widened. "A sex club?"

"Radiant."

"Radiant?" I repeated, throat drying.

My mind suddenly went completely blank, and I stared at her in shock. I thought … I thought Steven owned Radiant. I mean, his sister worked there, and he had access to private rooms. That had to mean something, right?

"Why do you look so pale?" Heather asked.

"Is his name Steven Patton?"

"No, his name is Hector," she said. "I've been chatting with him online."

"Hector?" I repeated because that was all I could seem to do tonight.

I racked my brain for that name, but I couldn't remember if I had ever heard it spoken at Radiant. My stomach turned, and I hoped that Hector wasn't really an online name for Steven because my little heart would be broken.

When I had been reading up on BDSM online, I had seen that some people used fake names or nicknames—especially at first—before meeting someone new. And honestly, I didn't know what to think.

And while I wanted Heather to have her own fun, what if … what if all this time, I had just been the stupidest girl in existence, thinking that Steven actually liked me because he was showing me some … favoritism in class?

I probably wasn't the only woman he was seeing. He owned a sex club!

Still, the thought wouldn't leave me alone. It was already so bad. I couldn't stop thinking about him. Now, this? I would spend the next week thinking about how my professor that I maybe, sorta liked could be banging my roommate!

Wanting to be civil—and not crazy—because Heather was one of my best friends, I leaned against the hallway wall and smiled. "Is this a *date*, date or a dick date?" I asked, attempting to be excited for her but also jealous as fuck.

She tossed her hair over her shoulder. "You'll know when I can't walk."

Turning around in the hallway, I sucked on the inside of my cheek.

Fuck.

Friday night, I would have to show up at Radiant—or his place —to see if Heather was really talking to him or to someone else entirely. Because if she was seeing him too, then I ... I would have to drop out of his class before I got too attached to him.

14

steven

FRIDAY EVENING, I sat back on the suede couch at Radiant with Michelle and Hector and rested one ankle on the opposite bouncing knee. I sipped on my wine and clicked my tongue against the top of my mouth, wishing Sierra would walk right into the club tonight.

While I didn't keep up with Sierra's social life—because why would I? She was my student and nothing more than that—the thought of her being at a frat party with handsy college-aged guys made my blood fucking boil.

"So," Michelle hummed, sipping her wine, "how is your class?"

"Good."

"Class?" Hector asked. "You're teaching?"

"Sex Ed," I said, cutting my gaze to Michelle. "*Someone* roped me into it."

"I did no such thing," she said, eyeing a regular at the wrap-around bar. "It's *just good*?"

"Just good."

"I've seen you a few times with one of your students," she noted, sipping on her wine and smirking at me. "What was her name again? Sierra, was it? How is she doing in class? Acing all your demonstrations?"

"Michelle," I growled in warning, "she's my student."

"Your student who"—she peered across the room in thought—"you haven't seen in five days now. It's been a long week for you, hasn't it? Is that why you've been an antsy, cranky, moody mess?"

"I have not been moody," I snapped and then immediately realized how moody that sounded. I took another sip of my drink and glanced away from the small group, gazing distantly at the occupied dancing poles. "I'm stressed from work."

"So, she has nothing to do with it?"

"No," I growled, attempting to find some excitement in watching the women dance.

But when I was into someone, I was fucking into them. No one else mattered to me. Not some swanky, naked women shaking their asses around poles for male enjoyment. I found no enjoyment in that. Absolutely fucking zero.

Hector gazed down at his watch and stood. "Well, I have a meeting to get to." He slapped me on the shoulder and leaned toward me. "Don't let her push you around. I have dirt on her, if you'd like to use it."

"What kind of dirt?" I asked, arching a brow.

"Get out of here," Michelle said, shooing him away. "You have nothing on me."

With a drink in his hand, Hector smirked and disappeared through the crowd. I blew out a breath and rested my head back onto the couch, closing my eyes. While I wanted to leave, too, and throw myself into work, I didn't want to go back to the office and stare at numbers for Radiant.

Maybe I'd take a stroll through Robinson's Giant Eagle Market District to see the hype.

"If Sierra doesn't have anything to do with your mood, then you wouldn't mind if ..." She glanced toward the bar, locked eyes with one of the dancers, and beckoned her to come to us. "Frazzy!"

"What are you doing?" I asked between gritted teeth.

"Helping you out," she hummed. "A girl will do you good."

"No," I growled.

"Frazzy, come here!" Michelle called over the music.

Frazzy sauntered over to us without clothes, swaying her hips back and forth and grabbing a wineglass from a waiter on her way over to the couches. I balled my hand into a fist and laid it on my thigh, glaring at Michelle.

I didn't want her to know that I hadn't been able to stop thinking about Sierra since Monday night, so I stayed glued to the spot and dared her to continue on with her little prank or joke or whatever the fuck she had been plotting.

Because she wouldn't.

"Hi, Steven," Frazzy purred, standing beside the couch and sipping her wine.

Narrowing my eyes at my sister, I didn't even want to look up at Frazzy. I had known her for almost a decade now, and I had never been interested in her even though she couldn't seem to stay away from me and made it a point to be here whenever I was.

"Loosen up," she said, walking behind the couch and setting her hands on my shoulders.

"Don't fucking touch me," I growled, sitting up and shuffling to the other end of the couch.

"But you're always so—"

When she went to place her hands on me again, I stood up. "I'm not fucking doing this."

"Does this mean that I win?" Michelle giggled.

"Piss off," I snarled, storming out of the room.

I grabbed my coat from Radiant's coatroom, barely shrugged it on before I slipped out a back door, and headed straight for my car. This stress had been from work, *not* from not seeing Sierra. She was a student who needed my help.

Nothing more.

But the thought of her wouldn't leave me the fuck alone.

Deciding that I needed to turn in for the night, I headed back to my place, parked in the garage, and walked through the lobby, straight for the elevators. I couldn't fucking believe Michelle.

After running my hand over my face, I tapped the elevator button and ran my tongue across the front of my teeth. I didn't want to wait until Monday. I had gone five long days without seeing her and had no excuse to invite her back to the club for a punishment or another class.

But when the doors opened, I stared at Sierra Monroe, holding a box of Swirl Scoops Ice Cream.

15

sierra

CLASPING a box of Swirl Scoops Ice Cream in my hands, I stared at the elevator floor. Well, I hadn't wanted to see Professor Patton anyway. He was probably with some girl like Heather and hadn't answered his door when I knocked because I had completely over-stepped our boundaries.

Being at Radiant was different than being with him in real life.

I should know better. I should fucking know better.

I stepped out of the elevator and frowned. Stupid me couldn't stop thinking about him all week, so much so that I had come up with the lamest excuse to buy a box of his favorite ice cream that I had eaten all of on Monday night and—

Someone stepped in front of me, seized the back of my neck, and moved forward, causing me to stumble back into the elevator. I yelped out and snapped my gaze up to the man as the elevator doors closed.

"Look what we have here," Steven murmured, pinning me to the metal wall.

My jaw fell open, and I attempted to shut it.

Fuck.

"I-I can explain," I said in my defense, holding the box of ice cream to my chest. "I wanted ... I was going ... I came to give you, um ..." My throat dried as I tried to find *any* excuse that would fit the reason why I was really here.

Come on, Sierra. You practiced this at home!

He curled his full lips into a devilish smirk. "What are you doing here, Miss Monroe?"

"I wanted to ... return the favor for letting me eat the rest of your ice cream the other night," I said, slamming the box right into his chest and hoping that he didn't see through my lame excuse of wanting to see him before the next class. "S-sorry."

It had either been this or show up at Radiant.

And I couldn't fucking do that. No way in hell. I had contemplated everything for the past few days and decided that heading to Radiant to see if Steven was Hector was a no-go. Plus, I didn't have the money for it. It would cost me literally an arm and a leg with its six-figure annual fee for members. Thank God that they had a huge— nearly free—educational program, or I would've *never* come here.

After grabbing the box from me, he arched his brow. "What's that look?"

"What look?"

"That one on your face."

"Were you at Radiant tonight?" I asked stupidly.

"Yes."

"Do you know ... Hector?"

He paused. "Yes. Why? Did he say something to you?"

"N-no," I said, glancing away. "I just thought that *you* were Hector."

Furrowing his brow, he narrowed his eyes. "Explain."

"My friend is at Radiant tonight, and she said that she is seeing the owner of the club," I whispered, cheeks reddening. Why the hell was I basically telling him how jealous and possessive I was? "I thought she was talking about you."

"Hector is my brother," he said. "Why would you think that?"

"Because ..." *I want you all to myself.*

"Miss Monroe, the polite thing to do is answer my question."

"Well, maybe I don't feel like being polite tonight."

He arched his brow.

I shrugged under his intense gaze. "I thought you only owned the place."

"It's a family business," he said. "I realize it sounds odd for a family to run a sex club together, but we're all adopted, so it's not that weird."

My lips curled into an O, and I swallowed hard, completely embarrassed and hoping that he didn't continue to push the subject because I honestly didn't know *what* I would say. I wanted him all to myself. Badly.

His lips curled into a small smirk. "Were you jealous?"

"No!" I scoffed and crossed my arms. "Of course not."

"Is that why you're really at my home?"

"No!"

"Bringing me my favorite snack?"

"Don't be ridiculous," I whispered, heart pounding. "I wanted to repay you. That's all."

"Well, how about you repay me by grabbing dinner with me then?"

Dinner? I wasn't expecting dinner!

"Oh, I, um …"

"Have you eaten yet?" he asked.

"Yes," I lied.

Cue the stomach growl.

He glanced down at my belly, then back up at me. "Are you lying to me?"

"No."

"Liars get punished," he murmured. "You do know that, right, Sierra?"

I sucked in a breath and nodded. "Yes, Sir."

Adrenaline rushed through my veins. I had come to his home on a Friday night to taunt him, blatantly lying to him while knowing the consequences, settling into subspace and calling him Sir like we were in some sort of BDSM relationship already.

Heat coursed through my body, my nipples taut at the thought of him punishing me. He had sorta, kinda done it after the first night of class, but he had held back. I knew he had. The way he had lit up with excitement when I talked about watching BDSM scenes, how he had ground himself into the mattress the entire time as discreetly as possible.

"*How* do liars get punished?" I murmured, my lips curling into a smile.

"I don't think you want to do this right here," he warned.

"Too scared to answer in public, Sir?"

"Take off your panties."

"No."

"Miss Monroe, don't start being a brat with me now," he said. "Take. Off. Your. Panties."

I stared at him through wide eyes, my heart racing and my cunt warm with pleasure. If I didn't obey him, then he was going to punish me. And I wanted to see what a punishment from Professor Patton was really like.

"Now, Sierra," he growled.

I teetered back on my heels. "I would, but I'm not wearing any."

16

"YOU'RE NOT WEARING ANY?" Steven repeated gruffly.

"I wanted to … surprise you," I said, completely embarrassed.

Before I had left my house, my stupid self had thought it would be sexy. Now, I was just—

"You're not wearing any underwear *because of me*?" he asked.

Voice hard. Angry. Furious almost.

I dropped my gaze. "I'm sorry. I-I overstepped. P-please don't be angr—"

"Fucking hell, Sierra," he growled into my ear, pressing his throbbing hard cock against my stomach and shutting me up. With his suit pants tight around the crotch, he cupped my chin in his hand and forced me to look up at him. "You can't say that to me in public."

My eyes widened from how hard he was without me even having to undress. All I had told him was that I hadn't worn any panties because I wanted to surprise him, and he felt huge. Like he was throbbing against me.

The elevator doors opened on the main floor once more, and I realized that we had never pressed the button for his floor. A group of people shuffled onto the elevator, and Steven gently nudged me.

"To the back."

After maneuvering between people, I stepped into the center of the back of the elevator as Steven slipped behind me and tucked the ice cream under his arm. I sucked in a sharp breath, wanting him to reach around and pinch my nipples between his fingers. They were so hard and aching.

When the doors closed, Steven placed one of his hands on my hips and dipped the other underneath my skirt from behind. I pressed my thighs together and sucked in a sharp breath, warmth exploding through my core.

He trailed his fingers up the curve of my ass, and I bit back a whimper. What was he doing?! We were in a cramped elevator with about fifteen other people around us. But if I whispered anything to him, everyone else would hear.

Before I could say anything, I pulled the back of my skirt up further and pressed my backside against him, his bulge nestled between my cheeks. Another wave of heat rushed to my pussy. I gently ground against him to tease him on the way up to his penthouse.

I could only imagine what he'd do to me when we reached his place. I'd bet he—

Steven shuffled behind me, pulled down his zipper, and pushed the head of his cock between my thighs, gliding it against my desperate pussy. I sucked in another breath and nervously glanced around the elevator.

Hoping to God that nobody looked over at us.

This elevator doors opened on the second floor.

He wrapped a hand around the front of my throat, dipped his head to brush his lips against my ear, and whispered, "Keep quiet, love, or else everyone will know that you're getting your pretty pussy pounded by a man twice your age."

A small whimper left my mouth, and I clenched.

Holy f—

After placing his free hand on my lower back to arch it slightly, he positioned himself at my entrance. I furrowed my brow, heart pounding in anticipation and pussy drooling all over his swollen head.

As the elevator doors closed, he pushed into me. I tightened around him and bit my bottom lip so I wouldn't whimper in front of everyone. But he was so big, stretching me out, and I couldn't get past the fact that we were doing this in public.

Right on an elevator.

With people around us.

Seizing my hips, he pushed his dick deeper into my cunt until my pussy lips were pressed against the front of his suit pants, completely ruining them with my juices. I balled my hands into fists, my nails sinking into my palms.

"I love the way your pretty cunt wraps around me," he murmured into my ear.

I clenched even tighter. And while I worried that others would see us, the thought sorta, kinda turned me on. It reminded me of class almost, and I wanted … for it to happen elsewhere.

Like at Radiant.

The elevator doors opened on the fifth floor, and a couple stepped out.

Steven took advantage of any noise or shuffling around, shoving himself faster into my sopping pussy. I squeezed my eyes closed and listened to the wet noises drifting through the quiet elevator. He reached around my torso and pinched my nipple.

A whimper left my mouth, and I stared down at the ground … or more like at his fingers on my breast, kneading and teasing my body through my clothes. He did it without any shame and as if he didn't care if anyone saw us.

When he took my nipple and tugged, the elevator dinged, and four people got off.

Once he started thrusting into me at a quicker pace, he slapped a hand over my mouth because I couldn't hold the cries back. One hand on my mouth, the other on my tit, he pounded into me quickly but as discreetly as he could.

But as soon as the last person stepped out of the elevator and the doors shut, Steven bent me at the hip, seized my hips tighter, and began thrusting into my pussy without mercy. I stumbled forward slightly, placing my hands on the doors and throwing my head back.

"S-Steven, th-the cameras."

"I have enough money to buy this building, Sierra. Don't worry about the cameras."

My pussy tightened around him, and I moaned.

When the elevator doors opened one more time, I threw my head back and screamed out in pleasure. We were at my professor's penthouse in one of the most beautiful buildings in Pittsburgh.

After grabbing a fistful of my hair, he tugged and continued to thrust. "Beg for my cum."

"Please, give me your cum!" I cried, pussy pulsing around him.

"Louder, Sierra."

"Please, give me your cum, Sir!" I begged. "Fill my tight pussy up with you—"

He slammed into me one last time and grunted heavily into my ear, "Fuck, I want to breed you so badly."

Heat coursed through my body, and I tipped over the edge again just from his words. Nobody had ever said that to me before. It sounded so dirty, so wrong, so filthy. Yet I couldn't stop myself from the eye-rolling, toe-curling orgasm that ripped through my body.

Instead of stopping like I thought he would, he pounded a few more times deep into my hole.

"Do you like the thought of having my cum dripping out of your little cunt every single morning when you wake up, before bed, while you're attending class?"

"Yes," I cried, legs trembling.

At this point, the only thing holding me up was his grip on my hair and on my breast.

And when he finally stilled, he pushed his cock even deeper. "Good girl."

The elevator doors began closing, but Steven pulled out of me and pressed the Open Door button to stop them. I collapsed onto the elevator ground, breathing heavily and closing my eyes. He picked me up and walked into his apartment.

"Th-thank you for the p-punishment, Sir," I murmured.

While I still didn't know the correct thing to say to someone experienced, I'd said what felt right and what I thought someone would say after receiving the best punishment in their entire adult life.

"Punishment?" He chuckled darkly. "Oh, love, you haven't seen punishment from me. That was merely because I couldn't control myself around you, especially when you showed up here for me. You'll get punished for not wearing any panties in class on Monday."

17

steven

"DO YOU KNOW WHAT TODAY IS?" I murmured, my hand around the steering wheel and my balls sitting heavy inside my pants. Since Friday night, I hadn't been able to get rid of my thoughts of Sierra and the punishment I would give her.

"My punishment," she whispered, grinding her thighs together.

"Do you know why you're being punished?"

"Because you asked me to remove my panties and I refused."

"No."

"Because I showed up at your place without any?"

"Ah, that's part of the reason," I hummed in amusement.

"But it's not all of it?"

"I'll give you one last try."

Honestly, she didn't deserve a punishment for showing up at my place without her panties. She had earned it for making me lose control in public and taking her pretty little pussy on the elevator with others around.

If anyone had seen me, I'd have been screwed. And never mind the headache I'd get if Michelle had caught us. God, I wouldn't have heard the end of it from her until the day I lay in my grave.

"Because I don't like being teased," I finally said when she didn't answer.

"I don't think that's much of a *me* problem," she said, staring at me through those lashes.

I came to a stop at a traffic light on Fifth Avenue and arched my brow at the mischievous glint she had in her eye. "You'd better watch that mouth of yours, love. Or instead, I'll punish you for being a brat."

"Do brats get punished harder?" she asked, batting her lashes.

When the light turned green, I tapped on the accelerator and glanced over at her once more. "The night you stumbled into Radiant, I didn't think you'd turn out to have a bratty mouth. I don't think you understand the extent of what my punishment could look like. You wouldn't be able to handle it."

She playfully crossed her arms and looked through the windshield. "I doubt that."

A chuckle rumbled through my chest. Little Miss Submissive over here wanted to play games. She'd be punished today, but I would hold back. No matter how much she thought she could take, she wasn't ready for true punishment.

And as much as I loved listening to her bratty responses, her mouth would be stuffed full with my cock tonight.

After I pulled into the garage underneath the building, I grabbed her hand and guided her toward the entrance of Radiant. She played with a hole in the end of her sweater, nervous. She finally had the confidence to talk back, but she feared the consequences.

As she should.

"After you," I said, holding the door open.

"What demonstration is today?" she asked, walking beside me to the class.

"You'll see."

"Please, can you—"

Before we entered, I grasped her chin in my hand and pressed her against the door, my body against hers. She sucked in a breath and stared up at me, letting me dip my thumb into her mouth.

"Don't talk back to me," I ordered, voice steady and strong.

She widened her eyes and didn't talk back to me the way I'd expected. I dipped more of my thumb into her mouth and let her suck on it as a reward.

"Good girl," I praised. "I won't be so hard on you today. And if you're good"—I pressed my hard cock against her stomach—"maybe I'll give you a reward after class. Would my girl like that?"

"Y-your girl?" she said on an exhale.

I didn't know why that had come out of my mouth, but I couldn't take it back now.

"Would you like that, love?" I repeated.

"Y-yes," she breathed, pupils dilating. "I would love that."

"What would you like as a reward?"

Without a beat, she answered, "For you to take a bath with me."

For a split second, I froze because I hadn't expected that. She had mentioned that she wanted to care for me after a scene, but I didn't see that as much of a reward for her. But, I stayed silent and grabbed her hand instead, pulling her into the classroom.

"Welcome to our class today, Throat Fucking 101," I said, releasing Sierra's hand and walking to the front of the room. "Tonight, we'll be learning how to fuck a woman's throat and how to have your throat trained for cock. Partner up."

Sierra shifted and scanned the room for a potential partner, as if she was still being that bratty little girl from the car, as if she wanted to test me tonight and act like she didn't already know that she was mine.

"Sierra," I called from the front, leaning back against my desk, my fingers curled around the edge and lips turned up into a smirk. "Looks like you have the pleasure of working with me again."

Instead of putting up a fight or trying to avoid working with me, she swallowed and nodded like the good girl she was and stepped forward. She dropped her gaze to the front of my suit pants and pressed her thighs together.

"No excuses today, Miss Monroe?"

"No, Professor."

I captured her throat in my hand and tugged her toward me until our lips were centimeters apart and her warm, minty breath was fanning my mouth. "I'd say that you don't know how hard that makes me for you." I strummed my fingers against the column of her throat. "But when I'm this far down your throat, you'll know."

18

sierra

A WHIMPER ESCAPED MY MOUTH, my cheeks burning. Steven didn't know how ready I was.

"Undress," he announced to the class, then turned to me. "Even you, Miss Monroe."

I swallowed hard and fiddled with the bottom of my shirt, then found the courage to pull it over my head as he watched me. When I unclasped my bra, his intense gaze didn't leave mine once, which only made the heat in my core rise.

Once I stood completely naked in front of him, he finally let his eyes fall to my body. He drew his tongue across his teeth, his bulge now stretching the front of his suit pants. He unbuckled his belt and pulled down his zipper, preparing to demonstrate to the class how to face-fuck one of his students.

"If you need me to stop and you can't verbally say your safe-word, squeeze my thumb three times. Okay?" he asked, and when I nodded, he placed one large hand on his desk and tapped it. "Up on my desk to start."

I slid up onto his desk and lay with my back against all his papers. He motioned to the side of the desk and commanded that I hang my head off of it and open my mouth. After shifting on the desk, I hung my head off the side and stared up at him.

"I'd like the women to follow Miss Monroe's lead," Professor Patton said. "Lie down on your desk, head hanging off the side of it, and open your mouth. We're going to start off by seeing how far your partner can slide down your throat."

Once everyone followed directions, Professor Patton slowly slid his dick inside me.

"You want to be able to see this bulge in her throat," he said, tracing the outline of his dick sticking against the front of my throat. He pushed his hips even closer to me, forcing me to take all of him. "And get it as far down as you can. She might try to push you away or pull her head back from this position, but you have full control of when you pull out of her."

Professor Patton grasped himself through my throat and began jerking himself off inside it. "Her throat will tighten around you and squeeze your cock almost as tightly as her pussy should."

He sank his cock into me until my lips pressed against his groin, and even then he began thrusting further and further down my throat to fill me up. Spit rolled down my face, ruining my minimal makeup, and then down into my hair. Between his dick all the way in my throat and his balls against my nostrils, I couldn't breathe.

When I pulled back for air, he didn't let me. "I control when I take myself out of you," he murmured. "We're training your throat, so I can fuck it whenever I feel like it, Miss Monroe. When I decide to pull out of you, you take one deep breath. That's it."

Heat rushed to my core, and I whimpered, desperate to breathe.

He reached over my body and cupped my pussy. "Do you understand?"

I nodded.

"Good," he said, then began rubbing my clit as he continued talking to the class. "Let her take a deep breath, then fill her mouth."

He pulled out just long enough for me to take a huge gasp of air, and then he shoved himself back inside me. He pounded into me for another thirty seconds, then allowed me to take one deep breath, then gave me his dick again.

Another deep breath, his dick.

Over and over.

Once he finally pulled out of me, my spit covered my face, ruining all my makeup I had put on to impress him tonight. He continued rubbing my clit, sending me higher and higher and higher. Then, right before I was about to explode, he slapped it.

I cried out in pleasure, waves of ecstasy rushing through me.

"Kneel in front of me, Miss Monroe," he ordered.

I scrambled off the desk, knelt in front of him, and stared up at him through the tears and strings of spit covering me. He moved one of his large, callous hands across my face, rubbing in the spit and drool, ruining me even more.

"If she doesn't look like a desperate, needy slut by the time you finish," Professor Patton said, "you didn't throat-fuck her hard enough, so you'll try again." He stuck four fingers into my mouth, opening it up enough to shove his cock back inside me.

Without hesitation, Patton slammed himself into me over and over, so hard and so fast that I grasped his thighs and dug my nails into his muscle.

"Let go of my thighs," he ordered. "Hands behind your back, like a good girl."

Following his orders, I put my hands behind my back and continued to bob my head on his huge dick. He loomed over me, one hand holding my hair back in a ponytail and the other pinching my nose closed so I couldn't breathe.

I deep-throated his dick, my mouth against his groin, and parted my lips, desperate for air. The more time that passed, the warmer my cheeks burned. I gagged and tried to pull away, but with his grip on my hair, he held me in place.

Tears built in my pleading eyes. "Please," I said around him, the word muffled.

"No."

"Please," I gargled.

"No," he said, voice harsher. "You can take it for longer."

Heat exploded through my clenching pussy. My aching nipples hardened against his thighs. Desperate for something, I gently skimmed my tits against his legs, the slight pressure shooting through my body—enough to hold me over for another moment.

"Longer," he demanded. "I'm not pulling away until you're choking on me."

When I couldn't take it any longer and my cheeks were burning, I coughed up spit on him and stared up at him through teary eyes. More and more drool rolled down my chin, my reflexes making me gag on him until I pulled my head back.

Once he finally let me go, more spit fell from my mouth and onto the tiled floor. I held my hands behind my back and looked back up at him, holding my mouth open and wanting more for some whorish reason.

One guy raised his hand. "What should we do if she gags and pulls away like that?"

Professor Patton took my face in his hands, then thrust his dick fast down my throat, hitting the back of it hard. Eyes wide and cheeks flushed, I gagged, pulled my head back, and coughed when he finally pulled out of me.

"Gagging like this," Professor Patton started, gently grasping my chin, forcing me to look up at him, and swiping his thumb across my bottom lip to wipe off some spit, "is no fault of her own. Just a natural reflex that you will have to train to get rid of." He stared down at me now, his eyes almost soft. "Because your mouth and your throat were made for sucking dick."

I nodded like the hungry fucking slut he had trained me to be these past few classes.

"But if she really can't take it and she keeps pulling away from you, you can place her against a wall," Professor Patton said, gently tugging on my shoulder to follow him to the wall.

I crawled over to it and placed my back against the wall, opened my mouth, and stared up at him.

He shoved his cock into my mouth again, ramming it deep down my throat. Reflexively, I tried to pull away again, but I had no space.

"She can try to pull back all she wants, but she's not going anywhere. Isn't that right, Miss Monroe?"

With his dick still in my mouth, I murmured, "Yes."

With one hand wrapped in my hair and the other massaging his cock in my throat, he gently rolled his groin back and forth against my lips. I stared up at him, swallowing around him and hoping that he liked it.

I rubbed my pussy, so close to coming but I was desperately holding off so we'd come at the same time. He'd see my eyes roll back in my head, and that'd tip him over the edge. I knew it would. Hell, I was surprised that he'd lasted this long.

"When you're about to come, you can pull out and come all over her face, or ..." Professor Patton kneaded his fingers faster against my skin, rubbing the head of his cock through my throat.

I furrowed my brow and kept my eyes open like a good girl, the pressure in my core building higher. Desperate for it now, I pushed myself even closer to him and sealed my lips around the base of his cock, cutting off the little air I'd had left to breathe and tipping me over the edge. My body seized in his hold, but I didn't pull back.

"Just what I was waiting for, Miss Monroe," Professor Patton said, tilting his head back and grunting. He came deep down my throat, filling it up with every last drop of cum that he had for me. "Or you can come down her throat and keep yourself there until she's forced to swallow it. My personal favorite."

I stared up at him through watery eyes, waiting for him to tell me that I could swallow. But the longer I waited, the more salty cum there was, pooling in my throat and my mouth. Feeling myself about to gag at the sudden pressure, I clamped my lips harder around his shaft and promised myself that if I did gag, I wouldn't let any cum out.

I would swallow every last drop.

"Don't stop touching yourself, Sierra," Professor Patton demanded, not moving his cock from inside me. He gripped my hair tighter to hold me in place. "You're not allowed to swallow my cum until you make yourself come again for me."

After whimpering on his dick, I pushed my hand between my legs again and continued to massage my sensitive clit. I furrowed my brow, staring up at him, unsure if I'd be able to make myself come once more. Everything was so, so sensitive.

He dropped one hand and fondled my breast, then captured my nipple between his fingers and pinched it. Pleasure shot through me, and I moaned, my legs beginning to shake. Once he released my hair, he did the same with my other breast.

"If you want to swallow, you have to come," Professor Patton said. "Do you understand?"

With the pressure building higher and higher inside me, I nodded. He kneaded my breast with his large fingers, then took my nipple again and pulled this time. A louder moan escaped my throat, and I rubbed my clit faster.

So close. I was so fucking—

"Come for me, my desperate little whore."

Pleasure exploded inside my core. My legs trembled uncontrollably. I swallowed his cum, threw my head back, and came hard. His hard cock fell out of my mouth and smacked against his thigh with a thump.

He captured my chin in his hand and swiped his thumb across my lower lip. "Great job today, Sierra."

19

steven

CANDLES FLICKERED around the room from the windowsill. Rain pattered against the large window near the bath. I turned on the hot water and filled the tub with Foamy bubbles for Sierra to relax after our session tonight.

"Take off your clothes," she said when the bath was half full.

"What?"

"Take off your clothes," she repeated. "You're coming in with me."

"Am I?"

"For aftercare."

I stiffened and swallowed, my palms clammy. "Maybe another time."

"But you promised," she whispered.

"I know," I said. "But ..."

She stared up at me through wide, sorrowful eyes, and I pushed all my insecurities to the side. I didn't want her to touch me the way I touched her because I didn't know how I would react to it for the first time ever.

"It's okay," she said after I didn't respond. She turned toward the bath and stripped off her shirt. "You don't have to do it today. Sorry for pushing it. Whenever you're comfortable with it, I would love for you to join me."

Once she stepped into the warm tub, I loosened my tie, then unbuttoned the cuffs of my shirt. She sat down on the side of the tub and stared up at me, eyes widening. When I undid all the buttons on my shirt and pulled it apart, a small smile graced her lips.

"You don't have to," she whispered.

I sat beside her on the edge of the tub, but instead of my feet in the water, like hers were, I pulled off my socks on the other side. And once I was finished taking off all my clothes, I turned around and sank into the tub with her.

When I finally settled back against one end, Sierra splashed some water on my hair, crawled into my lap, and straddled my waist. Then, she grabbed the shampoo bottle on the edge of the tub and squirted some into her palm. After giggling nervously, she massaged it into my hair, her pupils wide and a smile on her lips.

"Is this okay?" she whispered, peering down at me.

After placing my hands on her thighs, I nodded and closed my eyes. My body—and I—didn't know how to react to someone touching me so intimately.

Between my biological mother and all the shitty foster homes I had been in and out of back in England all my life, I hadn't had anyone to care about me when I was younger.

Even years later, I didn't really welcome it. Not with anyone else.

"You're so tense," she murmured.

When she placed her hands on my shoulders, they almost immediately relaxed under her soft touch. I had never once taken a bath with anyone before, never had my hair washed by anyone else, even when I was a child.

My bio parents had been too fucked up by drugs to care for their own child. I had despised them for so long for choosing to abuse pills and needles than to care for me, so much so that I had completely tried to shove them out of my mind.

But Sierra merely washing my hair fucking did something to me.

"I'm so sorry," she whispered, suddenly pulling back. "Did I do something wrong?"

"No," I said. "Why'd you stop?"

"Because ..." she said, her gaze dropping to my cheek. She pressed her lips together and settled back onto me comfortably, then swiped her thumb across my cheek. "Don't worry about it. It's nothing."

"What's wrong?" I asked, almost fearing her response.

"Nothing. Just use your safeword if you want me to stop," she hummed.

I chuckled and returned my attention to her. "My safeword?"

"*Unicorn,*" she hummed in amusement. "Did you forget it already, Professor Patton?" She clicked her tongue and shook her head in disappointment. "You know what happens when you forget your safeword, don't you?"

"What happens?"

"You get punished."

My arms came around her waist, and I pulled her flush against my body. The water sloshed between us as she wrapped her arms around my shoulders, her giggles drifting through my master bathroom.

"I thought I told you not to call me Professor Patton outside of the classroom?" I murmured into her ear, pushing some wet hair off her face. "Or *you'll* be the one getting punished tonight, Miss Monroe. Do you understand me?"

"Not if I punish you first."

A chuckle escaped my lips. "And how will you do that?"

Eyes wide, she attempted to formulate a response. But that cute little mouth couldn't come up with anything, except stutters. Her cheeks turned light pink, and she glanced away, playing with the ends of my hair.

"You know ... maybe I'll spank you."

"Spank me?"

"Really hard."

Another laugh escaped my throat. "If you slap my ass, I will spank yours until you're begging me to stop, love."

While I had called her the nickname more times than I meant to, she seemed to tense at it this time, her gaze dropping to my lips.

"Better watch yourself when you get out of the tub then," she said. "That doesn't sound like much of a punishment to me."

"Oh, it will be."

"Yeah?" she murmured, watching my lips move as I responded.

Fuck.

My heart pounded inside my chest, and I swallowed hard.

We stared at each other for a few moments, the only sounds coming from the crackling candles and the rain pattering against the large window that overlooked Pittsburgh. She inched closer to me, her gaze flickering from my eyes to my lips.

And then she gently cupped my face in her hands, leaned down, and kissed me.

20

sierra

STEVEN FROZE and didn't kiss me back.

And after a couple of moments, when the regret began setting in that I was kissing my Sex Education professor who was twice my age and obviously didn't want to kiss me back, I pulled back and looked away, completely embarrassed.

"Sorry," I said, attempting to regain my composure.

I didn't know what had come over me, but I had wanted to kiss him so badly. Maybe it was the way that he finally seemed to relax and joke around with me. Maybe it had been in a sexual kinda way, but it'd seemed much softer than usual.

"I'm sorry," I whispered again, finally scurrying out of his hold.

Before I could stand in the tub, he seized my waist, pulled me back to him, and crashed his lips onto mine. My heart pounded inside my chest as his tongue slipped into my mouth, and I curled my fingers around his muscular shoulders.

When he stood up in the tub with me in his arms, I wrapped my legs around his waist. Water dripped off our naked bodies and back into the soapy tub. He stepped out of the bath with me and walked toward his bedroom, decorating his hallway in wet footprints.

He kicked the master bedroom door open with his heel and headed straight for the bed, his hands gently kneading my ass. After setting me on the bed, he crawled between my legs with our lips still pressed together. I wrapped my arms around his shoulders and pulled him down closer to me, letting him slip his tongue into my mouth again.

Before I could grasp how quickly we had made it from the tub to the bed, Steven pressed the head of his cock against my entrance. I inhaled sharply and wrapped my legs around his waist, pulling him closer to me.

He placed his forearms on the pillow beside me and gently massaged the top of my head with his fingers. I pulled away, heart racing with anticipation as he ground himself against me.

Please, I mouthed against his lips.

Kissing me, he began pushing himself into me slowly. Then, he stilled.

It wasn't like him to take it slow by any means. He had forced me to strip naked and stolen my virginity the second day of class. So, this was ... different. Not in a bad way, but in a way that I had never experienced before.

And I loved it.

With slow thrusts, he pumped into me.

"God, you're perfect, love," he breathed, kissing up and down the column of my throat.

I tightened around him and curled my fingers around the curve of his shoulders, the pressure building higher and higher inside my core. A whimper left my mouth, and I arched my back, wanting him to push even deeper.

"So fucking perfect," he murmured against my lips. "I can't help myself."

"Don't stop," I said in a breathy whisper. "Please."

After squeezing my eyes closed, I held my breath almost instinctively to push myself higher. My pussy tightened around his cock, being pushed closer to the edge of the steepest cliff I had ever been upon.

"S-Steven ..."

"It's okay, love," he mumbled, resting his forehead against mine. "Let it all out."

When I cried out in pleasure, he plunged his tongue into my mouth, his strokes quicker, needier, and more desperate. I sank my nails into his bare back and whimpered into our kiss, my pussy exploding around him.

"Let it out for me," he whispered. "Just like that."

My skin pebbled, and another moan escaped my throat. "P-please ..."

I didn't know what I was pleading for, but whatever it was ... I needed it. Badly.

"It's yours," he murmured, grunting into my mouth and suddenly slowing to a complete stop with his dick deep inside me and his balls pressed against my entrance. "It's all yours, love. All yours."

And for some reason, his words tipped me over. I grasped on to him as tightly as I could, wrapping my arms around his shoulders and pulling him down to me to kiss him harder.

"All mine," I whispered into his mouth.

"Always."

21

steven

HEAD BURIED in something soft that smelled like strawberries, I curled my arm around a hard pillow and pulled it closer to my body.

It stirred in my arms, cuddling closer to me and whining softly, "What time is it?"

I slowly blinked my eyes open to see Sierra drifting in and out of sleep beside me. My body stiffened, eyes widening slightly. Had we fallen asleep together last night? I pulled myself away from her, sat up, and ran a hand through my hair.

I hadn't woken up next to a woman in years.

After sliding out of the bed as quietly as I could—because I planned not to wake her this morning—I hopped into the shower to make sense of what had happened last night. I had been completely in my right mind, but I … felt like I hadn't been. I'd let my emotions take control.

Once I finished and dressed for the day—all before my alarm even went off for the morning—I grabbed my belongings and headed straight for the bedroom door.

"Where are you going?" Sierra murmured from the bed.

I twirled around while tying my tie. "To work. I'll see you ..."

"Monday?" Sierra whispered.

While I didn't want to wait that long to see her again, I nodded because I didn't want to push her. She seemed way too riled up this morning, waking up in a different bed than her own. Or maybe I was just fucking making that up because I ... I didn't know how I felt.

Not after last night.

I hadn't realized it at the time, but I thought I had cried in the tub. And then Sierra had kissed me when I hadn't expected it, and I ... fuck—I ran my hand through my hair again—I'd kissed her back harder than I had kissed anyone before.

My heart swelled, and I gulped. "Yeah, Monday."

Before I could say something to her that I didn't want to say aloud, I turned around and headed toward the bedroom door. "You're welcome to stay here for as long as you want and eat whatever my cook will make you."

"Are you leaving now?" she asked, sliding out of bed.

Pausing, I stared at the door in front of me and hoped that I could clear my head by the time I made it to my downtown office today. I had meetings with Jeff about investments, networking with Michelle for Plaything Co. sex toys, and had to review plans for a new construction to provide housing for Pittsburgh families in poverty.

I couldn't be thinking about ... someone who wasn't even supposed to be my submissive.

Especially like this.

"Yes," I finally said. "I have a meeting at six."

Lie.

I needed to breathe. I didn't know what this feeling was inside me. I had never felt it.

"Is it okay if I ride down the elevator with you?" she said, pulling on her clothes from last night. I tilted my head slightly to peer back as her thumb caught in that hole in her sweater. She quickly fixed herself and smiled at me. "I have a long day too."

"Sure."

Fuck, why was I so awkward right now?

She must have sensed the sudden tenseness in my voice and paused. "Or if you don't want me to, I can take the next elevator down."

"Sorry," I whispered, opening the door. "Come on."

"N-no, I'm sorry." She turned her back to me and hurried to her backpack in the corner of the room, rummaging through it for her phone. "I shouldn't have stayed over last night. I hate when my roommate's friends overstay their welcome back at my place."

"Sierra …" I sighed softly. "I'm not angry with you."

When she turned back around, her hair fell into her face, shielding her eyes from me. She slipped past me and into the main living area of my high-rise, glancing out the window. "You don't want to be late. I'll catch the next elevator."

"Come with me," I ordered.

"N-no, it's fine. I will—"

I seized her chin in my hand and forced her to look at me, but when she did, her eyes were heavy with … tears? Everything I was about to say suddenly bundled in my throat, and I gulped it back down.

She didn't have to tell me. I knew exactly what that expression meant. I recognized it as one of my own that I'd had every day and nearly every night when I was just a boy, watching my parents drug themselves out.

Alone. Vulnerable. Unwanted.

Taking her hand, I tugged her through the foyer and to the elevator without another word. I didn't know what to say to her because I didn't want her to feel like that, but my damn emotions were all over the place this morning.

So, we rode down to the main floor in silence.

"Thank you," she whispered when we stepped out of the elevator.

"For what?"

"Letting me wash you last night."

After I guided her through the busy lobby, we stepped onto the morning streets of Pittsburgh. The sky was a white-gray, like it usually was every winter day, the sidewalks bustling with business people dressed in heavy coats and scarfs.

"I missed being able to care for someone," she said, staring distantly down the street.

"What do you mean?"

"I used to give my little sister baths and make dinner for my family before they …" More tears filled her eyes, and her lip quivered. She bit down on it to stop it from trembling and shook her head, laughing sorrowfully. "Oversharing again."

"Sierra," I said, tucking some hair behind her ear, "what is it? What happened?"

A bus pulled up to a stop at the corner, and Sierra grasped the straps of her backpack.

"That's my bus. I'll see you on Monday, Professor Patton." She hurried past me without another look. "Sorry again for overextending my stay."

22

steven

"I'M STEVEN PATTON," I said to the security guard inside of Sierra's building.

Dressed in the dullest gray uniform, he glanced up from watching a basketball game on his phone—full volume, mind you—and stared at me with an expression I could only describe as confused and disgusted.

"Is that supposed to mean something to me?" he asked, chomping on gum.

"Let me in."

He kicked his feet up onto the desk and continued on his phone, chomping on his gum. "Listen, I ain't telling you again. If you don't have a student ID or have someone check you in, then you're not getting in the building."

"What do you want?" I asked, pulling out my wallet.

Without glancing up from his phone, he laughed lifelessly. "For you to leave."

After balling my hands into tight fists, I shoved my wallet back into my pants pocket and stormed out of the building, heading straight for my car. I couldn't fucking believe this. I had come here twice in the past two days in hopes that they'd let me in to find Sierra.

And nothing.

Fucking nothing.

Once I slid back into my car, I stepped on the accelerator and headed down Forbes, swung back around onto Fifth Avenue, and made a beeline for Radiant. I'd really hoped that it wouldn't come to this, but I had no other choice.

It was Friday night. I hadn't seen—or heard from—Sierra since Tuesday morning, when I'd completely fucked up. What the hell was wrong with me? I had made it a point all my life not to make anyone feel the way I had when growing up. But my damn emotions had had to get in the way.

Now, she must've felt like the most unwanted woman in existence.

I parked in my usual spot and walked past the woman at the coatroom, not even bothering to drop off my coat. I wouldn't be here for long anyway. I would be in and out of Michelle's office in no time.

She didn't answer on the first knock, so I walked into her room and steered myself right for the filing cabinet. I yanked it open with my key and scanned the hundreds of folders for Sierra's name. They were all in alphabetical order, but Sierra's was missing.

Where the fuck did she—

"What are you doing?"

With a stack of papers in my hand, I twirled around, all disheveled. Michelle leaned back on her couch with one leg crossed over the other and a smirk on her face. She rocked her foot back and forth, the moonlight flooding through the window illuminating the red bottom.

"Nothing," I said, hiding the files behind my back.

"Nothing?" She playfully rolled her eyes. "Damn, Steven. You have it bad."

"I don't know what you're talking about."

Sauntering over to me, she grabbed the files from behind my

back, stuffed them into her cabinet, then grabbed one all the way in the back, where I would never have found it by myself. She extended the file toward me, and then when I went to grab it, she yanked it back.

"What do you need from it?"

"Her number."

"Oh my God," she said dramatically. "Ugh, you are terrible sometimes."

"What?"

"You've been fucking her for, what, three weeks now, and you don't have her number?"

Rubbing my forehead, I sighed. "Listen, I don't have time for this. I need her number. I can't find her anywhere, not her campus or her apartment. They won't even let me into the fucking building. I've tried twice. Twice!"

Michelle chuckled and flipped through the file. "Dick aching that badly?"

"No," I growled. "I fucked up."

Arching her brow, she looked up at me. "What'd you do?"

"It's none of your business, Michelle. Just give me her number."

She hesitated. "Did you ignore her safeword?"

"No, of course not."

"Then, what is it?"

I held out my hand. "Please."

Again, she rolled her eyes and placed the file in my hand. "You're terrible with feelings."

"Tell me about it," I mumbled, setting the file on her desk and finding Sierra's number.

Once I saved her number in my phone as a contact, I pressed the Call button but was immediately sent to voice mail. I called her again. And again. And again. All sent to voice mail. And on the last call, I drew my tongue across the bottom of my teeth, pacing.

"I've never seen you this way," Michelle said from her desk, leaning forward onto her elbows and kicking her legs back and forth underneath the desk. "Not even when you used to have regular dates. She must be special."

"She is." The words tumbled out of my mouth before I could stop them.

Michelle smirked, as if she'd just made me admit the greatest thing in my entire life. I gritted my teeth and stormed out of the office, slamming the door behind me.

Damn Michelle.

After I settled myself into my car, I texted her.

Me: Where are you?

Read receipt.

Me: Sierra.

Sierra: Who is this? How do you know me?

Me: It's Steven.

Sierra: Steven Patton?

Me: Yes, answer your phone.

I called her once more and *didn't* get sent to voice mail on the first try again.

"Hello?" she whispered.

"Where are you?" I asked, listening to voices in the background. "At a party?"

"No, I'm at the movies in Robinson with my friends."

"I want to see you."

She sucked in a breath through the phone. "You want to see me? I thought—"

"Please."

She paused, and I thought she was going to hang up on me.

"I want to see you too."

"You do?" I asked, eyes widening and a funny feeling bubbling in my stomach. "Really?"

"Only if you meet me at the Giant Eagle in Robinson," she said. "I'll be there in ten."

And with that, the line went dead.

23

steven

AFTER PARKING in the back of the lot of Giant Eagle Market District in Robinson, I buttoned the top of my topcoat and walked to one of the five entrances. Yes, five entire entrances for one store. I had driven around so many times, wondering which one was the correct one.

Deciding to enter through the flower section, I stepped into the warm building. I scanned the area for Sierra—the bar to my right. And when I couldn't find her, I headed toward the hot foods.

No Sierra in sight.

I stopped by the bakery, wondering how big this place really was. I didn't go to the grocery often anymore, but when I used to go as a kid, the store had barely been half the bar area here. And the bar area here wasn't even a tenth of the Market District.

Me: Sierra, where are you?

Sierra: I see you!

Arching a brow, I lifted my gaze and scanned the area again. Nothing.

Me: Where?

Sierra: Come find me.

Continuing my trek through the store, I passed the fresh seafood section, then the meats and veggies and fruits, which opened up into what had to be about forty aisles of everything. And I mean, everything.

They had about ten different types of Oreos, fifteen flavors of Ruffles chips, an entire animal food section, three people behind a counter to cut various amounts of cheese, a goddamn deli, and seven aisles dedicated to health and beauty.

I must've looked like a madman, pacing up and down the center of the aisles multiple times in an attempt to find Sierra. And when I finally looped back to the flowers, she was crouched in front of some succulents inside a snowflake-shaped vase.

"So, did you like it?" Sierra asked without looking up at me yet.

"You really had me walk down each aisle three times?"

She giggled, the sound making my stomach flutter, and glanced up. "I wanted you to get the full experience of grocery shopping for yourself at my favorite place in the world." She stood and placed down the vase.

"This place is too big to be a grocery store," I said.

"My family used to come here every weekend when I was younger," she said, smiling. "My sister and I would play hide-and-seek while my parents shopped. I'd hide by the barrels of coffee and nuts. And my sister"—she grabbed my hand and pulled me to the stairs that led to a seating area—"she used to hide underneath the microwave they have in the corner for people to heat up their food for lunch." She giggled. "Used to jump out at unsuspecting people, thinking it was me."

And while I had gotten all worked up, rushing around this store to find her, I smiled softly at her story. Usually, I hated all stories about families that Hector and Michelle had before we were all adopted, but hearing how happy Sierra was made me happy.

Even if it was only for a moment.

I sat down at one of the tables. "Do you have any other stories?"

"I do," she whispered, but then stopped herself and hid her face in her hair. "I have a lot of stories, but none that I really like thinking about often. But this place … it makes me happy, gives me only good feelings."

We sat there in silence for a few moments, and I admired the way her lips were curled into a small smile as she looked over the main railing and down at the fresh fruits and veggies section, cheeks rounded.

"I apologize for how I reacted Tuesday morning," I said, taking her hand and running my thumb across her knuckles. The guilt had eaten me alive this past week every single time I remembered the look on her face at the bus stop.

Sierra tucked some hair behind her ear and looked at the table. "It's okay."

I reached across the table to grab her chin and lifted it. "No, it's not."

She gently pushed me away. "It was my fault for staying."

"I wanted you to stay, but I … can't even remember the last time someone had slept over at my home, and I don't think anyone had given me a bath before you. I was nervous." *And scared as fuck because of the warm feelings inside my chest.*

"Nobody's given you a bath?" she hummed. "Not even your mom?"

After stiffening, I gripped her hand tighter. "No."

I didn't want to get into it and really didn't want her asking questions about it. Not right now. Having her over had been enough to freak me out. Letting her bathe me … that was enough for this week. I didn't know how *I* would react, telling her about my birth parents.

I hadn't even told Michelle and Hector the extent of abuse.

"Come," I said, taking her hand and standing. "I want to bring *you* somewhere now."

24

sierra

"WHY ARE WE AT THE MALL?" I asked.

"Because your clothes have holes in them," Steven said, taking my arm in his hand and showing me the hole that I usually played with in my sweatshirt. "I'm going to buy you some warm clothes for the winter."

"But—"

"Don't argue with me, Sierra," he said, pulling me into Luxe Room, one of the most expensive clothing stores in the mall. "Either you can pick the clothes out yourself or I'll buy you clothes that I want to see you wear."

After biting back a sigh, I followed him into the store and glanced around at the clothes that were *way* out of my price range. I hadn't even shopped here when my parents were alive and we had a little bit of extra money.

An hour later, Steven shoved his credit card back into his wallet and grabbed the three giant bags filled to the brim with new jeans, coats, sweaters, and long-sleeved shirts that he had forced me to try on. I had tried to get out of it by saying that I didn't like any of the clothes here, but he had taken control and nearly bought me half the store!

"Follow me," he said with one hand on my lower back to guide me deeper into the mall.

"But the car is in the other direction."

He continued and stopped near the escalators.

"Why don't we stop here?" he offered.

I paused in front of Birch Jewels and chewed on the inside of my cheek. Maybe he needed to buy a couple of diamond-encrusted watches or … something for him because if he thought he was going to buy something else for me in here …

He had another thing coming.

"Is there anything specific that I can help you find?" a woman said when we walked in.

"Necklaces."

"Steven," I scolded quietly, grabbing his elbow, "no."

Ignoring all my pleas, he took my hand and followed the woman to the cases to the left with diamond bracelets and necklaces. I ripped some skin off my inner cheek and nervously played with the end of my sleeve.

"Do you like any?" he asked.

"Steven," I whispered, glancing at the diamonds and jewels, "these look expensive."

"Do you like any?" he repeated.

Nerves bubbled up my stomach and into my chest. "H-how much are these?" I asked.

The woman grinned. "These average about eighty."

"Eighty dollars?" I asked, sighing a breath of relief.

"Eighty thousand."

My hand snapped around Steven's, and I turned on my heel toward him. "No."

"My treat."

"This isn't a treat!" I whisper-yelled. "These are eighty-thousand-dollar necklaces!"

"Pick out one that you like," he said nonchalantly.

Like eighty grand meant nothing to him!

"But—"

"Sierra, please," he said, as if he didn't want to argue.

Wanting to choose the least expensive one possible, I glanced down into the case. I hated taking other people's money. Heather's parents always bought me nice things for Christmas and my birthday that I hated accepting. And I'd tried to repay them for the apartment multiple times too.

My gaze landed on a simple choker-style diamond necklace toward the back. None of the others really fit my style, and I wasn't someone who wanted huge diamonds on my neck to show off to everyone.

"Do you like that one?" Steven asked.

"It's nice."

"Just nice?"

"I think … it would fit my style the best."

He pointed to the same one in the back. "Let's try this one."

"Ah, lovely," the woman exclaimed. She walked around the cases and unclasped the diamond necklace. I pulled my hair out of the way and swallowed hard as she fastened it around my neck. "This is one of my favorites!"

Once she stepped away, I gazed into the mirror and then nervously up at Steven.

"Leave us," he said to the woman.

And while nobody would even *think* about leaving someone my age alone with a piece of jewelry that cost eighty grand or more, the lady nodded and walked into a back room. He stepped behind me in the mirror, his gaze on my neck.

"Do you like it?" he asked.

"It's okay."

"If you don't like how it looks, there are others."

"No, Steven," I whispered. "That's not what I mean. It's expensive."

"I asked if you liked it. Not if you think it's expensive."

"You've already bought me clothes," I said. "That's enough. Let's go."

"Sierra," he said, his voice stern.

I sucked in a breath and snapped my gaze to his, feeling the warmth pool between my thighs. He only used that commanding tone when he wanted me to obey him during sex. But this ... this was so much money.

And I didn't deserve it.

"I'll never be able to repay you," I whispered, chest tightening. "Please."

"You don't have to repay me."

"But—"

"You want to repay me? You can give me another bath."

My eyes widened. "But you don't like baths. Last time that happened ..."

Tuesday morning drifted through my mind, and I swallowed hard. My stomach had been in knots all week as I thought about that morning, wondering what had gone through his mind and what had even possessed me to sleep over at his place.

"I really enjoyed it," he said. "Nobody had given me a bath before. Do we have a deal?"

"Are you sure?"

His lips curled into a smile. "All I want is a bath as repayment."

"A bath it is." I glanced at the diamond choker around my neck. "One expensive bath."

He moved closer to me and brushed his fingers against my shoulder, following my gaze. "Do you like this one? If you don't, we can try a couple of other places or even order a custom piece for you."

"No," I said, because a custom piece sounded even more expensive. "This is perfect."

"Good," he said, smiling. "Because you'll be wearing it often."

25

steven

SIERRA WALKED out of the Cathedral of Learning alone with her hands wrapped around the straps of her backpack and a small smile on her face when she spotted me. I kicked myself off my car, shoved my phone into my pocket, and dropped my gaze to her bare neck.

"Where is your necklace?" I asked, grabbing her backpack from her.

"Oh, it's back at my apartment," she said.

"Do you not like it?"

"I just don't want it to get ruined tonight during class."

"I want you to wear it," I ordered, careful not to say more.

I wanted her to wear it to her classes, to her internship, while she was out with her friends, and especially while I had her bent over my desk at Radiant because when any other man even *looked* in her direction, I wanted him to know that she was taken. By me.

"What if it gets ruined during class?" she asked, chewing on the inside of her cheek.

"Then, I'll buy you a new one."

"That was eighty grand!" she exclaimed. "You're not going to buy me a new one."

"Well, if you don't wear it, then I'll be purchasing a new one for you."

"Steven!"

"Get in the car, Sierra. We're going to pick up the necklace before we head downtown."

After pursing her lips at me, she slipped into the passenger seat. I shut her door and then drove us a few blocks down Fifth and parked outside her apartment building. I wanted to come in this time.

Once I found parking, I grabbed Sierra's hand and marched to the entrance.

"You again?" the security guard sighed. "Didn't I tell you to get your ass outta here?"

Sierra glanced between us. "I'm signing him in."

"Bitch," he said, holding a hand to his chest, "I know you're not signing *him* in."

When Sierra nodded, he rolled his eyes in the most dramatic way possible, grabbed my ID card, and scanned us both into the building. I followed her toward the elevators near the security guard table.

"What'd he mean?" she asked. "You haven't been here before."

"Actually ..." I drew my tongue across the tips of my teeth. "Long story."

"We have time," she said, pausing at the elevator.

"I ... might have visited this building on Friday night ... looking for you."

She bit back a giggle. "*You* were the harasser?!"

"The harasser?"

"Bobby told me that some guy had been harassing him Friday night, asking to get into the building when he didn't have a proper ID." She clutched her stomach and laughed. "Said that he was a minute away from calling the police on you and that you threatened to set him on fire."

"Okay, okay. The first part might've been true, but I *did not* threaten to set him on fire."

She arched her brow and stepped onto the elevator. "You sure about that?"

"I wanted to," I mumbled. "For stopping me from seeing you."

When we reached the fifth floor, the doors opened. I followed Sierra through the maze of a hallway to apartment 509. She tapped her key card on the lockpad and typed in a code, and then the door clicked. She swung the door open and flickered on a light.

"This is your place?" I hummed, walking into the small but luxurious apartment.

"Sorta," she said. "It's more like … my roommate's place, and I live with her."

I followed her into her bedroom and sat on the bed. Damn, how'd she sleep on this?

She grabbed her necklace from a drawer.

After adjusting to the hard mattress, I glanced around the room and spotted a picture frame hanging up on the wall. "Is this your family?" I asked, lips curling into a small smile.

They all looked so happy together, and part of me was envious of her for how privileged she was to have even taken that picture with her family. How she could call her family at any time to hear them say that they loved her.

She glanced over my shoulder as she buckled on the necklace and smiled softly, tears building in her eyes. "Yeah."

"What's wrong?"

"Nothing."

"Sierra," I warned, "you have a family that loves you. What's wrong?"

"I *had* a family that loved me," she said, lips quivering. "They're gone now."

Before she could run away into another room or convince me that we'd be late for class, I grabbed her elbow and pulled her back to me. "What do you mean, they're gone? What happened to them?"

"Steven," she whispered, "I'd rather not talk about it right now."

"Sierra, I—"

"Steven, please. We're going to be late."

I swiped my thumb across a stray tear that had rolled down her cheek. "Okay, let's go then."

Once we returned to the car, I opened her door and then slipped into the driver's seat, starting the engine.

"We have an exciting class tonight," I murmured, watching her heavy eyes brighten. "One you're going to enjoy."

"Is it another punishment?"

"No," I said, arching a brow. "You enjoyed the punishment?"

She bit back a smirk. "No, *of course not.*"

"I'll ignore the sarcasm in your response," I hummed. "You get rewarded tonight."

"For what?"

"For wearing your col—necklace without being a brat to me."

"Just for wearing this?" she murmured, drawing her fingers against the diamond necklace we had picked up in her bedroom.

I nodded.

"What's my reward?" she asked.

"Patience, Miss Monroe. Patience."

26

MASTURBATION 101 WAS WRITTEN in chalk across the board.

I eyed the class name from the doorway and slowly walked into the room, eyes on Professor Patton, who had walked ahead of me to the front of the class. Heat gushed between my legs. When I made it to my usual seat, Professor Patton smirked at me with that handsome face of his.

"Sierra," he purred, voice low and sultry, "I told you that you'd enjoy it."

"Are you going to use me as your demonstration again?" I asked, leaning forward in the desk.

"As my demonstration?" he asked, placing a single finger under my chin, lifting it. "You're going to teach the class tonight."

More warmth pooled between my thighs, my pussy clenching. "Wh-what?"

"You're catching on to this material so well," he hummed.

"B-but how can I teach guys how to … to get off?" I asked, glancing around at the mix of females and males in the classroom today.

If we were learning how to masturbate, then I couldn't teach a bunch of guys! I didn't have a dick.

"Most of these guys have been jerking off since they were in high school," Professor Patton said, gently moving his hand across my shoulder and squeezing. "They don't need you to teach them how to get off."

"Then, why are they here?" I asked shyly.

"Because, Sierra, it's not every day they get to watch a beautiful woman touch herself."

Swallowing hard, I pressed my thighs together and peeked around at the other students again. Nerves bubbled up inside me. Sure, I had fucked Professor Patton in front of them before, but I had never been the center of attention like this.

"Come," Professor Patton said, walking to his desk. "Up here. Class is about to begin."

When the students quieted down, I slowly slipped out of my seat and headed to the front of the class. Professor Patton placed a hand on my shoulder, his fingers curling around my arm and making me warm in all those sinful places.

"Tonight, Miss Monroe will teach the girls how to touch themselves," he announced. "This is a hands-on experience for everyone involved, so get comfortable and watch Sierra make"—he dropped his voice—"her little pussy feel good."

Pleasure shot through my body at the mere sound of his voice. I swallowed my nerves and shimmied out of my clothes until I stood in front of the class in nothing but a set of lacy black lingerie and my diamond necklace. Professor Patton leaned against my empty desk with his huge arms crossed over his chest, watching my every move.

"Be a good girl, Sierra," he said. "You know you should be naked."

"Or what?" I found myself saying before I could stop myself.

Professor Patton cocked a brow. "Or we will push this class to a later date, and I can teach everyone how to punish a bratty little mouth like yours. Is that what you would like, Miss Monroe?"

My heart raced as my cheeks flushed, nipples hardening through my bra. His gaze dropped to them for a second, then to my thighs pressed together.

"You want to be punished harder," he concluded. "Noted for a future session."

I whimpered softly, my panties soaked through already, and unclasped my bra so my breasts fell out of it. Then, I pushed down my underwear to my ankles and stepped out of them. I shuffled back onto his desk nervously.

"Go ahead, Sierra," he said. "Teach us."

"Do you want me to"—I swallowed—"just … touch myself?"

"I want you to show us how you finger that dripping cunt while you're home, alone."

Brow furrowing, I reluctantly posted my feet on the edge of the desk and spread my thighs so everyone could see just how wet my pussy was, like Professor Patton had said. My gaze flickered around the room, watching the other women copy my movements and the guys undoing the button of their jeans.

Then, I looked over at my professor, gaze falling to the front of his pants.

To his throbbing bulge.

Another whimper escaped my lips, and I slipped my hand between my legs. My fingers moved across my clit, back and forth, rubbing in small circles. The pressure rose in my core, my empty pussy clenching on nothingness.

"Don't look at me, Sierra," Professor Patton said. "You're here to teach the class."

Gulping, I shifted my gaze from him to the class again as I watched everyone touching themselves now. I rubbed my cunt even faster, heart pounding inside my chest. I so desperately wanted to look back over at him now, wanted to touch myself to him.

Especially when he kicked himself off my desk and moved closer to me.

"We're going to add a toy," he murmured, digging around in his desk drawer.

Like he had demanded, I continued to rub my pussy and kept my gaze on the class. The guys were stroking their dicks, and the other girls were getting themselves off … *to me*. Which only made me wetter.

Professor Patton walked around the desk with an eight-inch-long, three-inch-thick dildo in his large hand. I stared at it through wide eyes and clenched my tight pussy, heart pounding.

"You're going to put that inside me?" I squeaked. "It's way too big."

"Nothing is too big for this pussy," he said, cupping my mound in his free hand and sticking two fingers inside me while I continued to rub myself off. He let a wad of spit drip from his full lips to the head of the toy. "Let me prove it to you."

When he drew it between my pussy lips, I whimpered. Inch by inch, he slowly pushed it inside of me, stretching my tight hole. I stopped rubbing my clit and stared up at him through wide eyes, brow furrowing.

"Professor …" I whimpered.

"Take it like a good girl."

I clenched again, clamping down on the toy and wishing he were inside me.

But at least for this class, he wouldn't be.

This was Masturbation 101, not Fucking 101 again.

Once about four inches were buried inside me, he stopped and peered down. "Your fucking pussy takes cock so well," he growled, dark, hooded eyes gazing upon me. "Tell me to push it deeper."

"Push it deeper, Professor Patton," I breathily whimpered. "Please."

He pushed it another inch deeper and grunted. "The way your pussy lips spread and swallow this toy whole, Sierra"—another inch—"it gets me hard as fucking hell," he growled, then slammed the rest of the toy into me.

I threw my head back and cried out in pleasure.

When he finally stepped away, his dick pressed hard against the front of his suit pants. I clenched on the toy and readjusted myself so the bottom of the dildo pressed against the desk and the toy stayed deep inside me.

Unable to stop myself, I moved up and down on it while I rubbed my aching clit. The pressure rose so high in my core, and I wasn't sure if I was supposed to come yet, but I was damn close to letting it all go.

He disappeared from my view once more to grab another toy from inside his desk.

"Open your mouth," he ordered, standing behind me.

I tilted my head back slightly and parted my lips, mind hazy from the pressure inside me. He slipped a dildo gag into my mouth and fastened it around the back of my head. My eyes widened slightly, drool already pooling in my mouth.

"How do you like it, Sierra?"

Spit falling out of my mouth, I nodded and furrowed my brow, a muffled moan escaping my lips. I gripped on to the edge of the desk with my free hand and rubbed my clit even faster, my pussy dripping with pleasure.

"If you'd like, you may partner up," Professor Patton announced to the class, fastening two nipple clamps on my breasts that were attached by a thin chain. He pulled on the chain, and the clamps tugged on my nipples. "But no penetration."

Partners began forming, but I couldn't focus on the class anymore as he stepped between my legs and gazed down at my body. He rubbed himself off through his pants, swallowed, and then undid them, whipping out his cock.

I moaned when I saw how hard it was. I had seen his cock countless times before in the class, had it inside me, but I ... I couldn't help but get off on the thought of him sliding it inside me again. Right here. Right now.

God, I need it.

He spit on the head.

Badly.

He wrapped his hand around the base and slowly stroked it.

So fucking badly.

Before I knew it, the head of his cock was millimeters from the entrance of my pussy. He let out a shaky, deep breath.

"No penetration," he repeated to himself, stroking his cock faster. The head of his cock rubbed against my wet pussy. "No fucking penetration."

"Please," I whispered, words gargled and inaudible, "put it inside me."

The dildo was already thrust as deep as it could go, but I wanted to be filled up even more. I wanted him inside me, thrusting in and out of my pussy as quickly and as hard as he could, pounding away, making me his.

He clenched his jaw in an attempt to control himself, but with his free hand, he harshly tugged on the nipple clamps.

I sputtered out in pleasure. "Please! Please put it inside me!"

"Sierra," he gritted out, almost as a warning.

I rubbed my pussy faster, drooling all over my tits.

Stroking himself faster, he unclasped the gag and ripped it from my mouth in an almost-animalistic manner.

"I touch myself and think about you every night," I breathed out, moving my fingers quicker. "I bury my fingers between my thighs and scream out your name, Professor Patton." I furrowed my brow. "I can't stop thinking about you. Please, put it inside me."

"Sierra," he growled, pressing his dick directly below my clit.

"I get off to you coming inside me," I pleaded. "You filling my pussy up with your cum."

When he pulled the dildo out of my pussy, I sucked in a sharp breath and waited for him to shove himself inside me. But instead, he grunted, his warm cum shooting all over my spread pussy lips and the head of the dildo.

"F-fuuuuck," he groaned.

Curling my toes, I teetered on the edge. And when he slammed the dildo back inside me, shoving his cum deeper and deeper and deeper until it reached my cervix, I threw my head back and screamed out in pleasure, unable to hold back any longer. Ecstasy shot through me, my eyes rolling back into my head and my entire body shaking.

"Good job tonight, Miss Monroe," Professor Patton said, pushing himself back into his pants. "You've been a good girl for me today."

27

sierra

ONCE I HAD COME multiple times on Steven's desk, I stumbled out into the hallway as all the other students left for the night and Steven cleaned up my mess in the class. I leaned against the wall with my eyes closed softly and breathed out.

"Sierra, right?" Michelle, Steven's sister, said.

"Yes," I said, gazing at her. "If you're looking for Steven, he's—"

"Cleaning up?" She giggled, then dropped her gaze to the necklace that Steven had gotten me at the mall on Friday night. "Oh, wow. This is beautiful." She drew her fingers across it. "Did Steven buy that for you?"

I didn't want her to think I was using him for his money because I wasn't, and I had tried hard to get him *not* to buy me something so expensive. But I also didn't want to lie to her because I didn't want Steven finding out.

"I didn't ask him to," I whispered, cheeks warming.

"So, he's collared you."

My brow furrowed. "What's that mean?"

She parted her full lips, then lifted her gaze behind me. "You should ask Steven."

"Sierra," Steven called from behind me, closing up one of the back rooms, "you ready?"

After Michelle threw me a smile, I said my goodbyes and followed Steven to the back exit near the parking garage. The drive back to his place was quiet, and I wasn't sure when—or if I even should—bring it up to him. But I finally decided it was a conversation for another night when I slid into the bathtub with him.

Halfway into our bath, I shifted in the tub and crawled into Steven's lap. I grabbed the shampoo and squirted a bunch into my palm so I could wash his hair. After wetting it, I drew my fingers through his locks.

"Sorry for kinda freaking out when you asked about my family earlier," I whispered.

He placed his hands on my hips and squeezed, slowly opening his eyes. "It's okay. I get it. Talking about family is hard. But you can always talk to me about it. I'm not going to judge you, Sierra."

My lips curled into a frown, tears building in my eyes. "My family is dead."

As soon as the words left my mouth, I became paralyzed to the spot, my fingers stiff in his hair, my mouth half open, and my torso flexed in a weak attempt to stop myself from sobbing uncontrollably. I had tried so hard to get over the memory, but I hadn't healed past it.

Not yet.

"A drunk driver hit their car in December of my senior year of high school, causing them to run off the road and into a freezing river. They were turning onto my street, bringing home Christmas gifts they had gotten for me."

A tear rolled down my cheek. Maybe one day, I'd get through it. But not today. Not soon.

"God, Sierra," he whispered, wrapping his arms around my waist. "I'm sorry."

"I watched from the house… It happened right in front of me," I said, voice breaking. "Right in front of me, Steven."

"Love," Steven mumbled into the crook of my neck.

"It should've been me," I cried. "I should've been in that car too."

"Don't say that."

"It's true," I sobbed, doubling over and grasping on to his shoulders. "I wonder every night why the world is so cruel. I loved them so much, Steven. So much, and I will never see them ever again."

Steven held me tighter to his chest as I bawled my eyes out.

"I had gotten in a fight with my sister right before she left, and I told her that I hated her." My body shook uncontrollably in the water, tears and snot running down my face and into my mouth. I cried out in pain at the memory. "I'm a terrible sister. A terrible sister."

"You're not a terrible sister," he murmured.

"I am."

He gently took my chin in his hand and forced me to look at him through my burning, stinging, tear-filled eyes. "From all those stories you shared with me at the store, you are not a terrible sister. You didn't wish this on your family. You were frustrated, but you still loved her."

My hiccups filled the large bathroom, and I tried to calm myself down by grasping tightly on to his shoulders and hoping that Larissa would think the same thing. I had never forgiven myself for what I'd said to her.

"Please," he said, holding on to me tighter, "don't for a second wish it were you."

"It's hard. So hard sometimes, Steven."

———

Once I finished sobbing and finally dried off from the bath, I pulled on my clothes from today and headed toward my backpack that I'd placed on his king-sized bed. "I should probably get going. I have a long day tomorrow, and I know that you do too."

He snapped his gaze up to mine. "Do you want to stay?"

"No, it's okay. I don't want to—"

"Let me clarify." He placed his phone on the dresser. "You are staying."

"Okay," I whispered because I wasn't going to argue.

Although I appreciated that Heather's family was well off enough to pay for our housing, I hated having them pay for everything, so I had bought my own mattress, which felt more like a brick than comfy. Steven's bed was so soft that I sank right into it.

I peeled off my more restrictive clothes and my necklace, setting it on the nightstand, and then I climbed into bed and pulled the blankets over my bare shoulders, waiting for him to join me and to cuddle—though I wasn't sure he would.

While Steven finished preparing for bed, I rolled onto my side so he couldn't see my phone and typed *what does collaring mean in sex* because I couldn't get the thought out of my head since Michelle had said something to me earlier.

A few BDSM websites popped up in the search. I nervously glanced at Steven to make sure that he couldn't see—because I didn't want him to think I was searching something that I might not even be into—then clicked on the first link.

After I read through the article three times, the bed dipped beside me, and Steven slipped underneath the sheets with me. I quickly shut the phone off and hid it underneath the pillow so the light wouldn't glare in the darkness.

I turned onto my back and stared up at the dark ceiling.

Collaring a submissive meant commitment.

Did that mean that I was the only person he was seeing and interested in seeing right now? We spent more time together than he did with anyone else in the class, hopefully. But did this mean *serious*, serious? Just last week, he'd freaked out that I had slept over. And I didn't have to wear the necklace at all times. Only during class and when we were together. Did that mean something? Or maybe he did expect me to always wear it.

Only one way I would ever find out. I'd have to ask him.

28

sierra

"DO you know anyone just like me?" Annabella asked, holding my hand in her smaller one and staring up at me through huge hazel eyes. She pushed her tongue between her missing front tooth.

"What do you mean?" I asked, guiding her toward the playroom with the other kids during work the next day.

"Someone who doesn't have a mommy and daddy?"

Tears welled up in my eyes, but I held them back. "I don't have a mommy and daddy." I crouched down in front of her and shook away my thoughts of them. That was not what she had asked. I took her hands. "But one of my really great friends grew up without a mommy and daddy. He is just like you."

"Really?" she asked, lips turned into a frown.

"Really," I said.

"Does he have a lot of friends?"

"I—" I paused. "Why?"

"Toni at school says I won't ever have a lot of friends because I don't have a family."

"Don't listen to Toni," I said, intertwining my fingers with her small ones. "You will have tons of friends, just like my friend does."

"What's his name?" she asked.

"Steven."

"Do you like him?"

My lips curled into a small smile. "Of course I like him! He's my friend."

She wiggled her eyebrows at me. "But do you liiiiike him?"

"Miss Annabella," I hummed.

She pinched my rounded cheeks between her fingers and giggled. "You do!"

I stood back up and took her hand. "All right, time to go play."

Once I ushered Annabella into the playroom, I blew out a low breath and pushed away a tear from my cheek. I loved working here with these kids to show them the love that my parents had always given me, but working with children in foster care was difficult.

Kids said the saddest things sometimes.

After grabbing my things from the back room, I shrugged on my coat and walked out the doors to head back to my apartment, a short walk away. I pulled out my phone and noticed a message from Steven.

Steven: Be ready at six.

My eyes widened slightly, and I walked down the sidewalk past a couple of football players.

Me: Why?

Steven: I'm taking you to Market Square for the holiday market.

My lips curled into a soft smile as I checked myself into the building and headed for the elevator. *Steven wants to take me to Market Square?! In the middle of the week? On a ... date?* I shook my head. *Surely not.*

Me: What if I already have plans tonight, Mr. Patton?

Once I hopped out of the elevator, I opened my apartment door.

Steven: Be ready at six.

After glancing at my phone's clock, I dropped all my belongings on the counter and ran to Heather's room.

She stood at her mirror, holding up two lacy lingerie sets to her body. "Do you like pink or purple?"

"Purple," Athena, one of our friends, said from the bed.

"You guys have to help me," I squealed. "I think he just asked me out on a date."

"Shut up," Heather said, dropping both lingerie sets and running for her makeup. "Finally!"

Nerves bubbled in my stomach, a giddy feeling rising in my chest. But was it really a date, or did he just want to fuck me afterward? I looped my thumbs around the ends of my sleeves and smiled softly to myself. Either way, we were going somewhere outside of Radiant.

Together.

She shoved me down onto a makeup chair. "Don't move," she said, moving a mascara wand close to my face.

Just as she was about to plunge it into my eye, I jerked back and squinted. "Heather!"

"I said not to move." She grabbed my chin to steady it and moved the brush closer to my eye again. "I'm not going to hurt you. Just don't pull away." She snickered. "Just like you don't with Mr. Professor Man."

Once she finally finished my mascara ten minutes later, she opened my jewelry box and skimmed through it, glancing from me to the contents inside the box. Then, she pulled out some small diamond earrings.

"Did he buy you this?" she asked, staring at my necklace.

"Yes."

"You wear it a lot," she hummed. "Did he buy it for you as a collar?"

I pressed my lips together, thinking back to when Michelle had asked me the same thing.

"What's a collar?" I asked, wanting clarification. "I mean, I looked up the meaning but ..."

Part of me still wasn't sure, and I didn't really want to ask Steven because what if I was wrong and it really wasn't a collar, but a nice necklace? I guessed they were sorta the same thing, but—*gah*—all this new terminology was really confusing me.

"Basically, a collar is a commitment to submit to a dominant," she said. "Usually."

"Usually?"

"Well …" She sucked in her cheek. "If yours is a collar, I don't know why he didn't tell you about it or explain what it was. Hector said that his brother has never officially collared anyone, so maybe he's not into it?"

Steven hasn't collared anyone?

Michelle had said it with so much confidence that I thought that this was a thing for him. But maybe not. Maybe he had just wanted to buy me something nice. Then again, he had been so concerned when I wasn't wearing it for class.

"Has Hector collared you?" I asked.

She rolled her eyes. "He's making me earn it."

"What does that mean?"

"Hector enjoys absolute dominance," she said. "He told me that in order for him to even consider collaring me, I would have to stop being so bratty and submit to him." She playfully rolled her eyes. "And he wants me to be healthier."

I chewed on the inside of my cheek and reached up to play with the necklace.

"By the way, my mom wants to know if you're bringing a date to our Christmas party."

I fiddled with the end of my sleeve and stared at my thighs. "No."

"No?! You're not going to ask your sexy professor?" she hummed. "Hector said that he's British?! Why the hell didn't you tell me that he's freaking British, Sierra?! That's, like, the first thing that should've come out of your mouth!"

"I'm not going to ask him to come with me," I said. "We're just casual."

She arched a brow at me. "Buying someone a diamond necklace isn't casual."

"Yeah, but ..." I glanced in the mirror at Athena on the bed.

"Tell her, Athena."

"Do it," Athena said. "Ask him to come."

"Ask him to come," Heather cheered. "Besides, Hector is going to be there."

"You're bringing Hector to your parents' Christmas party?!" I exclaimed.

What would her mother say if she found out her daughter was dating someone twice her age who owned a BDSM club down-town?! She had to either be crazy or she loved the thrill of possibly getting caught.

"He's my dad's best friend," Heather said.

My eyes bugged out of my head. "*That* Hector?! The one your mom kept calling *Hec*? I remember him from last year's party."

Goddamn, they weren't related biologically, but the Pattons had adopted some attractive kids.

"Yes, the sexy Hector," Heather said, wiggling her brows. "You have to bring Steven."

"That means I'll have to ask him," I whispered.

"Duh."

"Heather!" I said. "It's not that easy."

"It's, *Hey, Sexy Professor Man, come to a Christmas party with me and then fuck me afterward.*" She giggled. "It is literally that simple. Men are not as complex creatures as you think, Sea."

Athena snickered from the bed. "She's right. That's all it takes."

"We're more complex than that," Charlie—who I hadn't seen until now—said, waltzing into the bedroom and sitting beside Athena on the bed.

Charlie and Athena had been best friends since freshman year of college.

Athena playfully rolled her eyes. "Please."

"You think I'd be convinced to go to a party if promised sex afterward?" Charlie asked her, his brown eyes wide, like a puppy dog's.

They stared at each other for a few moments, Charlie giving

Athena playful eyes while Athena *attempted* to be uninterested. I glanced at Heather in the makeup mirror and bit back a smile because we both knew they secretly had a thing for each other.

But Charlie was too good and too sweet to make the first move.

"Anyway," Heather said, curling her finger around a strand of my hair, "you'd better invite him tonight or else."

"Or else?" I giggled. "You're not too good at threats."

"Shut up." She laughed, setting her hands on my shoulders. "You're done."

I nervously stared at myself in the mirror, heart racing at the thought of finally going on my first date since that idiot who I now called my ex-boyfriend. My lips curled into a smile, though my stomach was tight in knots.

Tonight, I'd have to ask Professor Patton to Heather's Christmas party.

29

sierra

OUCH!

I snapped my mouth away from the sizzling hot chocolate in my cup after it burned the first layer of tissue off my tongue and shrank down in the winter coat that Steven had bought me the other day. Steven sipped his with ease beside me as we walked through Market Square.

"Do you come here a lot during the winter?" I asked, rubbing my cold fingers on the cup.

"Since I moved my business into that building right over there" —he pointed to one of the tall buildings near Market Square—"I've always wanted to come down and check it out in the winter, but I haven't had much of a chance."

"Why not?" I asked, inching closer to steal his heat.

"Because I"—he paused—"have never had anyone who would go with me."

My eyes widened, and I bit back my small-talk response of, *Oh, really?* Instead, I opted for the embarrassing and clichéd, "Well, I'm happy to go with you anytime you'd like! I haven't been down here much either."

Dressed in a dark gray topcoat, he glanced over at me with those amused eyes and smiled softly. That look did something to me, my stomach feeling fluttery and light. I brought the cup up to my lips again and forced myself to take a sip.

A band played Christmas music in one of the corners, the main singer dressed as Santa. I gazed at all the expensive gifts, ornaments, and jewelry that vendors were selling and continued through the crowd, Steven's fingers slipping around mine.

Another wave of excitement rushed through my body, and I squeezed his hand. *Is this really happening in front of everyone right now? What does it mean? Is this a date, like I thought it was?*

"Are you hungry?" he asked.

"A bit."

"I have a reservation for us at seven thirty at Alta."

"Alta?" I asked, gazing up at him. "Where's that?"

Once we made it out of the crowd and to the main street, where a car had been waiting for us, he pointed across the river to a tall mountain that overlooked the city. My gaze drifted from the Duquesne Incline to the restaurants with large windows.

After a fifteen-minute drive, our driver pulled to the curb in front of Alta. Butterflies fluttered through my stomach at the thought of Steven even making this reservation for us, never mind it being at a fancy restaurant.

I had sneakily texted Heather in the car, asking her if she had been there before, and she had started freaking out and telling me that this really was a date with my BDSM-loving billionaire Sex Ed professor and that I needed to ask him to go with me to her family's holiday party.

Which I had been building myself up for.

But then Steven had completely knocked me off-balance, wanting to bring me to dinner.

Steven took my hand and helped me out of the car, his hand

falling to my lower back as he guided me toward the entrance, where someone took my coat. I watched the attendant disappear into the back room in surprise.

Besides at Radiant, I hadn't been anywhere where they took my coat during dinner.

"This way, Mr. Patton," the hostess said.

When we stepped into the main dining area, I pressed my lips together so my jaw wouldn't drop open at the prettiest sight of Pittsburgh that I had ever seen through the large floor-to-ceiling, wall-to-wall windows.

We sat near the window at a table with about a billion different forks. I smoothed out a napkin on my lap, nervous that I'd do something wrong in front of all these ritzy, rich people here. Because I didn't know the first thing about forks!

"It doesn't matter which one you use," he said, watching me stare at the silverware.

"But they're all different."

He chuckled. "They're forks. They all do the same thing."

My lips curled into a smile, and I relaxed against the back of my chair, sipping on some champagne that they had brought over to us. Steven smiled back, his cheeks tinting red just a smidgen, and sipped his champagne.

Did Steven Patton just blush?!

Oh God, that smile did something to me …

"So," I said once we ordered, "my roommate's family is hosting a holiday party."

The champagne must've been strong tonight.

"Oh, yeah?"

"Yeah."

I stared at him, expecting him to know what I desperately wanted to ask him, but when he didn't answer, I nervously looked away. My cheeks burned, and I played with the ends of my sleeves.

"And she wants me to bring someone."

A smirk crossed his face. "Oh, yeah?"

"Yep."

"And?"

"And I don't have anyone to go with."

"Are you trying to ask me on a date?" he hummed. "Because you're terrible at it."

"No!" I exclaimed, burying my face in my shoulder. "I am not trying to ask you on a date."

But I totally was.

"Hmm," he said, opening his calendar on his phone. "Looks like I'm free anytime you need me. But if you're not trying to ask me out on a date, then I guess I'll have my assistant book those meetings—"

I grabbed his hand and stared at him, heart racing. "Please."

While I expected him to force me to explain what my pleading meant, force me to ask him to Heather's family's party, he bit back a small smile. "Of course I'll go with you, love. And because you asked so sweetly"—he gently cupped my chin—"next class, you'll get a reward."

30

sierra

NEXT CLASS, Steven seized my waist in his strong hands, lifted me into the air, and set me on his desk so I faced the class. My skirt rode up my thighs, barely covering my soaked panties. He tapped my left knee, wanting me to spread them.

I sucked in a sharp breath, still so embarrassed in front of the class. They had all seen me naked, and some had even fucked me. But I still wasn't confident in myself, still didn't know if I looked weird or awkward, like Luke had told me.

"Spread your legs," Professor Patton ordered.

"Wh-what are we doing today?" I whispered.

"Clit Stimulation," he murmured. "Then, I get to eat your cunt until you're crying for me."

Heat exploded through my pussy. "Really?"

"Spread. Your. Legs. This is your reward, remember?"

From merely the tone in his voice, I inched my legs further apart and stared at the class, who had already gotten into partners, though nobody had followed Professor Patton's lead yet. I swallowed hard and gazed at him.

Once he slipped between my legs, he slid his large hands up my thighs. Goose bumps rose on my skin, my pussy dripping in anticipation. He bunched my skirt up at my hips and gazed down at my sheer panties, then pulled them off me.

"All right, class," Steven said, pulling out two toys from the desk drawer, both from the Plaything Co., "today, we're learning about why it's important to stimulate your partner's clit and how to do it. Girls, up on your partner's desk."

Professor Patton handed me a Plaything Co. wand vibrator and took the three-by-eight dildo we had used during the last class. A wad of spit dribbled from his lips onto the head, and he used it as lube to make it wet and slippery.

I spread my legs further apart and leaned back onto my forearms, nipples hard.

After he moved it back and forth over my clit a few times, he dropped the head a couple of inches lower and pressed it against my entrance, teasing and taunting me with the dildo until my pussy was wet and desperate.

My fingers dug into the wooden desk, and I whimpered, "P-please ..."

Inch by inch, Steven pushed the toy into my cunt. I stretched around the phallic object, my pussy adjusting to the large size, and moaned when the palm of his hand pressed the last inch into me, the toy nearly against my cervix.

But I desperately wished that it were *him* inside me.

"Hold this inside of you gently, Sierra," Professor Patton said. "Don't let it fall out."

I lightly placed my hand on the button of the toy so it wouldn't pop out of my pussy.

"Her pleasure is your own," Professor Patton said to the class, grabbing the wand from the desk beside me. "Always stimulate her clit because it doesn't just make her feel good, but ... *watch*."

Professor Patton handed me a wand vibrator and turned it on the third-highest setting, then placed it at the top of my cunt, right where my pussy lips parted. I tightened just a smidgen, but when he moved the vibrator lower to my swollen clit ...

God!

My pussy clamped down on the dildo, clasping it as tightly as it could. Completely unintentionally. The dildo moved deeper inside me for the entire class to see. And then when he pulled the vibrator away, I relaxed around it.

"This is when you're inside her," Professor Patton announced, gesturing to the way my pussy gently clasped the dildo. He placed the vibrator against my clit again. "And this is when you stimulate her clit. Look at how tight that pussy gets."

He pulled the vibrator away again, letting me relax.

Then pressed it to my clit.

Pulled it away.

Pressed it to my clit.

Over.

And over.

And over.

"Sir!" I cried out, lying flat on the desk now and clawing into it. "P-please!"

He chuckled. "I know you're desperate for it, but I'm teaching a class, Miss Monroe."

"Please," I moaned, the pressure rising higher and higher in my core. "I can't handle it anymore." I reached for his wrist and pulled the vibrator back to my clit, pressing it hard against my swollen, sensitive bud and throwing my head back. "Oh my God!"

Steven moved the vibrator in small circles around my clit, a dark chuckle escaping his lips and his sinful gaze slithering up my body to the diamond necklace around my throat. I brushed my fingers against it and came hard and fast on his desk.

"She becomes a dirty mess when you toy with her clit," he announced. "Look at her."

My legs jerked into the air, and I pulled them to my chest, whimpering.

As I slowly came down from my orgasm, he placed the vibrator down on the desk beside me and pulled the dildo out of my pussy, replacing it with his fingers. He dropped down to his knees at the base of the desk and pulled my legs onto his shoulders.

And then he ate.

Pressure and pleasure surged through me, my clit more sensitive than it had ever been.

I grasped my necklace, feeling nothing but ecstasy.

"Professor Patton," I whispered, chest heaving, "wh-what does my necklace mean?"

He stared up at me through his brows and spread my pussy lips apart with his fingers, his tongue flicking over my sensitive clit repeatedly. I arched my back and moaned softly, desperate to hear the words roll off his lips.

"Is it a collar?" I asked.

A low growl escaped his mouth, and he sucked my clit between his lips. Hard. Another wave of heat rushed through me, and I reached down to push on his shoulders. Not because I wanted him to leave me alone, but because the pressure was suddenly building.

I squirmed in his hold, afraid that I wouldn't be able to come like this. He had made me come in so many positions, so many ways, but my mind was buzzing with what this necklace meant. He hadn't answered me yet.

Would he even answer me at all?

"I'm sorry," I whispered. "I don't know if I'll be able to—"

Before I could finish my sentence, pressure pooled in the base of my core. I curled my toes and stared down at his mouth sucking on my clit. His lips were latched on to my cunt, his hands holding my thighs apart.

He gazed up at me, as if daring me to continue my sentence. I had apologized so many times during the first night of class, when he had brought me into one of those glass rooms and forced me to touch myself for him.

At that time, I didn't think I'd be able to do it myself, but he now dared me to say that *he* wouldn't be able to make me squirm, scream, and come; that he didn't have what it took with his mouth;

that he wasn't willing to eat my pussy for hours, days even, to satisfy me.

"Professor!" I cried out in pleasure, grasping the back of his head with both my hands and pressing my cunt against his mouth. Pleasure exploded through my core as my legs trembled uncontrollably.

"The necklace," he mumbled against my clit, "means you're mine."

31

steven

AFTER EVERYONE STEPPED out of class, I helped Sierra pull her clothes back on and gave her privacy to gather her belongings. I needed to find my damn sister because we had a big fucking problem.

I caught a glimpse of her freshly dyed purple-brown hair across the bar and stormed toward her, grinding my teeth. She flirted with Frank Freddrick, a regular at the club, and one of his few wives.

"Oh, look who it is," Michelle said, smiling at me. "How was class?"

"Fucking great," I said, snatching her elbow and pulling her to the side of the room.

On our way, she downed her drink and set it on a table, where someone was bound to knock over the glass.

"What the fuck did you tell Sierra?"

Michelle played dumb and twirled her finger around a strand of her hair. "Oh, nothing."

"Diamond necklace? Collar? Does that jog your memory?"

Someone had told Sierra about collars, and I would've bet that it was Michelle. It had to be.

"I just asked her if the diamond necklace you make her wear during your class is a collar," she said, placing a hand on her chest. "I don't think the poor thing even knew what it meant. Did she ask you about it?"

I gritted my teeth. "It's not a collar."

"Mmhmm."

"It's not."

"And you two aren't a couple then?" she asked. "You wouldn't mind if she explored a bit more with other doms who might want to collar her? Because if not, I saw Frank staring her down when she walked in with you earlier."

My head snapped to Frank, who stood at the bar, watching Sierra at the door. I balled my hands into fists and gritted my teeth. While Frank respected boundaries, there was no fucking way that I would let him near her. Not a fucking chance.

"Exactly what I thought," Michelle said.

After turning back toward Michelle, I pressed my lips together. "I've already told you a million fucking times, Michelle. The answer is not going to change anytime soon. I'm not ready for that commitment."

"You already bought her a diamond necklace," Michelle said. "I know what it's worth is like pocket change to you, but you've never done that. I want you to be happy, Steven, for once in your life. Stop being scared."

I stared at her and ripped off some skin on my inner cheek. "I'm not scared."

I was fucking terrified.

What if Sierra decided that I wasn't worth it anymore and walked out of my life, like every other woman had? They were all gone, and I didn't want Sierra to be another one on the list. I didn't want to—I couldn't—lose anyone else.

Michelle looked me up and down, then let out a breath. "It's okay to be nervous."

"You don't understand," I said, staring at the ground. "It's hard."

Michelle frowned. "I bet it'd be harder without her."

Sierra stood by the classroom door, glancing around Radiant. When we made eye contact, she smiled softly, and my chest tightened. I didn't want to be hurt again. I wanted to ignore all the pain, all the emotions that I had ever felt.

And just fuck.

I dropped my gaze as the thought drifted through my mind. It was a lie.

A damn lie that I had been drilling into my head since forever.

"Maybe you should invite her to Christmas dinner," Michelle offered.

"I can't do that."

"Why not?"

"Because ..." I started, attempting to find a reason why I shouldn't invite Sierra to Christmas dinner.

She didn't have a family to celebrate with either. Had she been spending all these holidays alone?

"Invite her!" Michelle said, walking back to her friends and tossing a smirk over her shoulder at me. "Or I will."

Once she settled back into a conversation with Frank, I dropped my gaze and clenched my jaw. I couldn't do this. I couldn't fucking do this. Sierra was mine, but I was ... scared to tell her the real reason for the necklace, the real reason I had crawled into the tub with her, the real reason I liked her being around.

"Steven," Sierra said, grabbing on to my elbow from behind, "are you staying here?"

I swallowed my nerves, straightened myself out, then grabbed her hand. "Of course not. I still need to clean and feed you."

"Are you sure?" she asked. "You look distraught. Did something happen?"

After wiping the stress off my face, I shook my head and guided her toward the exit near my car. "Don't worry about it, love. I'm going to run a bath for us while Thornton makes us dinner. I'm going to take care of you tonight, like I always do."

32

steven

I PUSHED a cart down an aisle at Giant Eagle, following Sierra to the cheese section the night of the Christmas party at her friend's house.

Thank God that she hadn't brought up the necklace again because I wasn't sure what I would tell her. I wasn't ready to be in a relationship, and I honestly didn't think I would ever be at this rate. I didn't want to deal with the consequences. With what was fated to happen.

She'd leave at some point.

"You should shop for your own groceries," she said.

"I don't have time, love."

"You make time for me."

A bubble of laughter tumbled from my stomach, my body light. "That doesn't mean I have time to shop for my own groceries. I have Thornton for that. He does all the shopping and cooking while I work. Besides, I have never met anyone who likes grocery shopping."

"It's relaxing for me," she said, walking down the aisle toward the pickles and smiling. She drew her fingers across all the glass jars, never stopping to pick one up, but continuing toward the ketchups and mustards.

My lips curled into a smirk as I remembered the story that she had shared with me the last time we came here, when she and her sister would play hide-and-seek inside the store and scare unsuspecting people.

She headed straight for the wide variety of cheeses without a care in the world, pausing at the selection of wheels. She hummed softly to herself, glancing at the precut cheese in the coolers.

I wondered who she would be spending the holidays with. Part of me wanted to ask her, but what would I say if she was spending them alone?

With five blocks of cheese in her arms, she walked back over to me and dumped them into the cart. "Follow me," she said, walking toward the meats and seafood sections. Her high ponytail bounced up and down as she walked.

I didn't want her to spend it alone, but would she even want to spend the night with me? I never saw any of my family on Christmas Eve; I would spend it alone at Radiant, which was usually dead.

"What kind of wine do Heather's parents enjoy?" I asked once we picked up sliced meat and salmon and headed for the alcohol.

I gazed at the shelves. None of these would do as a gift. We'd have to pick one up from my wine cabinet back home before we left tonight.

"Oh, they will have tons of it."

"What're you perusing the alcohol for then?"

"To find the kind that I like," she said, plucking a bottle of Afterglow from the shelf.

Once she placed it in the cart, she grabbed the back of the cart and hopped onto it while I pushed her to the checkout. People glanced over at us, throwing Sierra weird looks but she didn't seem to mind it.

It was probably something that she and her sister used to do here.

Once we checked out, I stared out the glass windows at the pouring rain and frowned. "Stay here."

"Where are you going?"

"To get the car."

"I'm coming with you."

"It's pouring, Sierra. Stay here."

She snatched the full cart from me and pushed it right out the sliding doors and into the sideways-falling rain. I cursed, pulled one of the paper bags to my chest, and followed after her, wanting to get to the car quickly before the rain soaked through our clothes.

With one foot on the bottom bar of the cart, Sierra propelled herself forward with her back leg and hopped onto the cart with both feet. The carriage glided forward on the wet pavement.

"Sierra!" I shouted, jogging after her. "You're going to get hurt."

"Live a little," she said, her voice drifting over the loud thumping of rain between us.

The cart picked up speed near the car. She attempted to stop herself at the car, but her foot slipped on the wet pavement, and both she and the cart continued rolling down the parking lot toward the grassy area. Sierra tried to catch herself, but she tripped once more.

I dropped everything in the middle of the lot and ran toward her. The cart crashed into the grass, the contents spilling everywhere, and she fell over onto her stomach in a puddle on the concrete.

"Are you okay?"

Sierra grabbed my shoulders and pulled me down toward her, giggling like a maniac. I fell down onto the concrete with her in the middle of the pouring rain and caught myself before I slipped into the puddle beside us.

"Sierra, I told you to be careful."

"I'm fine," she said, her voice soft.

"We're lying at the end of the parking lot in the rain," I commented.

"You know, I don't know if I've ever seen you laugh for real."

"I laugh all the time."

"Whenever you laugh, it's always so serious," she said, giggling behind her hand. "I mean, one where you're clutching your stomach and laughing so hard that nothing comes out and you can barely breathe."

"You shouldn't be laughing until you can't breathe, love."

"Something's wrong with *you* if you don't laugh like that, *Steven*."

"We should go." The rain had already soaked through my shirt. "We don't want to be late."

But Sierra didn't move. Instead, she stared up at the gray clouds.

"When I was younger, my dad used to let me jump on the back of the cart while he jumped on the front. And we'd roll down to our car. My mom would hate it, but it was the highlight of my childhood."

My lips curled into a small smile. Rain poured down on us and the pavement, the heavy drum of splattering drifting through my ears. I rolled onto my knees and grasped her hands to pull her up so we could get out of this storm, but she lay on the concrete with her lips trembling.

"I miss my family," she whispered, staring up at the gray sky. "So much."

After dropping her hands, I lay down beside her and stared up at the sky, my fingers intertwined with hers. I couldn't relate to her in the slightest, but I didn't want her to be upset. She was mine to take care of. And sometimes, that meant lying in the rain with her while she cried her eyes out.

33

sierra

"SORRY THAT WE'RE LATE," I said, walking into Heather's house.

"Sierra!" Heather's mother, Ms. Hodge, exclaimed. "You brought a boyfriend."

Heather's mom and dad had divorced years ago, but they were still on good talking terms with each other for Heather and celebrated the holidays as a family, which I was always so, so jealous of.

I stiffened and glanced up at Steven. "He's just a friend."

Steven squeezed my hand. Hard.

Ms. Hodge smirked at our hands. "Seems to be a little more than just friends, but never mind that." She turned to Steven and furrowed her brow, looking him up and down. "I know you from somewhere, don't I?"

Please don't say Radiant. Please don't say Radiant. Please don't say Radiant.

"I'm Hector Patton's brother," Steven said.

"Hector and my ex-husband are business partners and the best of friends," she said. "That must be it."

After she grabbed the bottle of wine that Steven had convinced me to bring over and the cheese platter that I had made earlier, she ushered us into the house and toward the living room, where people mingled together.

"Didn't think you'd be here," someone said from behind.

I twirled around to see Hector Patton walking up to us, his gaze on his brother.

"This is Sierra," Steven said, introducing me to his brother. "Sierra, this is Hector."

"We've met before," I said. "I've seen him at Heather's mom's party."

"Ah, yes," Hector said, about to say more. But then glanced past me to Heather, standing near our friend group in the corner by the piano. She wiggled her brows in our direction, but I wasn't sure who she was flirting with. Me or Hector.

"I'm gonna say hi to my friends," I said, looking at the group.

"Charlie?" Steven said, eyeing the tall blond Goody Two-shoes of my friend group.

"You know Charlie?" I asked.

"A bit," Steven said. "He attends Radiant."

Interesting.

I walked toward the group, giggling at Heather still giving Hector *the eyes.*

"Does your Dad know?" I asked. "About you and Hector?"

"Of course not!" Heather exclaimed. "Do you think I'm a masochist?!"

"Maybe." Athena chuckled from the couch. "You're crazy."

"I am not," Heather hummed.

And while she might not be medically insane, she had signed up for a BDSM club to lose her virginity to her father's best friend and business partner. If that didn't scream a bit on the weird side, I didn't know what else could.

"So, Sierra, you're sleeping with his brother. Is Heather right? All the Patton genes are good ones?" Athena winked and sipped on her champagne.

"Athena, they're both adopted."

She playfully rolled her eyes. "You know what I mean."

"Don't think she does," Charlie said, lips curled into a smile. "Why don't you explain it?"

Athena shot Charlie a playfully dirty look, then shoved a dessert into his mouth. "Shut it."

"What?" Charlie said, mouth full of cookie. "I didn't say anything wrong."

"You're trying to embarrass me," Athena said.

Charlie finished chewing. "You're trying to embarrass her."

"Yeah, but Sierra's cute when she's all flustered."

"So are you."

Athena turned a deep red, and the rest of our friend group looked at each other. Athena and Charlie were the best friends in the group that refused to admit that they even liked each other, but then they *both* said stuff like this.

A while later, Steven brought me a glass of wine. I lifted it to my lips, preparing myself for the bitterness of alcohol because I had already downed all the wine that I liked, but when it hit my tongue, it was even sweeter.

We slipped outside onto the small balcony that overlooked the acres of land that Ms. Hodge owned. While I envied Heather for still having her family around, I always noted that her family's home never felt homey, like mine had.

Neither did Steven's, but I'd assumed that was for other reasons.

Snow drifted from the dark sky and blanketed the yard. There were no swings or slides or toys scattered across the grass. No scuffed floors from small sneakers. No pictures of Heather when she had been younger. No homeyness.

"How're you feeling?" he asked.

"Good."

"Even after the parking-lot cry?"

I had cried for so long in Giant Eagle's parking lot that I made us late, and I hated being late. But I couldn't help it. I had made an entire fool out of myself in front of him because I'd let my memories get the best of me.

My chest tightened. Why had I done that?

I glanced away. "Sorry you had to see that. This time of year really gets to me."

He pushed some hair behind my ear. "I'm not here to poke fun at you, love."

Heart racing, I looked up at him. "You don't think I'm crazy?"

"Why would I think that?"

"Because I burst out into tears for no reason."

"It wasn't for no reason," he murmured. "And I know that."

"Luke used to think that I was crazy," I whispered, crossing my arms over my body and thinking about how low he had always made me feel when I thought about what had happened with my family. He had told me that I shouldn't think about them because they made me sad.

"Forget about him. He's a dick."

A small giggle escaped my mouth. "I know but …"

"It's hard," he finished, gaze dropping for a moment, as if he was thinking back to a memory. "It's hard to love and be loved. To get past all the trauma that's happened to you. To be okay again."

Tears built in my eyes, but they wouldn't fall. Steven was speaking everything that I felt.

"Sometimes, you just have to let go," he murmured. "What're you doing for Christmas?"

The question had come so suddenly, his tone changing within seconds.

"Usually, I come here," I said, dropping my gaze as my chest tightened.

I used to love Christmas, but since my family had died, I had come to loathe it.

"They welcome me, but I always feel like I'm intruding on family time."

"I spend Christmas Eve and morning alone," he said. "Do you want to stay at my place?"

With my gaze still fixed on the ground, I widened my eyes slightly and played with my sleeve. "I, um …" I swallowed hard and peered up at him through my lashes, nerves zipping through me. "If you don't mind, I would love that."

He let out a breath, as if he had been holding it in. "Great."

"It's a date then," I said.

"The first Christmas that I've ever looked forward to."

34

steven

NEXT CLASS, I parked in the alleyway just outside of Radiant and led Sierra toward the entrance of the club. I had been buzzing every night and every day since the holiday party. She had promised to stay the entire week—from Christmas Eve to the day after New Year's Day.

While I should've been nervous because I had never had anyone stay over my place for that long, I couldn't seem to wait. Lately, my home had seemed so boring without her. I had found myself lounging around every night, staring down into the quiet city and wondering how much longer I'd have to endure the agony of being alone.

I tightened my grip on Sierra and pulled her hood up before we stepped onto the searing cold sidewalk from the alley. She giggled, her cheeks already a light pink, and quickly looked away, as if she wanted to tell me something but was too embarrassed.

"What is it?" I asked.

"What?"

"Why do you have that look on your face?"

"I don't have a look." She snickered, stepping into Radiant.

With my hands on her hips, I pulled her closer to me before we walked through the second set of doors and dipped my face into the crook of her neck. "You have a look, love. I can tell when you're hiding something from me." I curled my fingers into her sides. "Don't make me tickle it out of you."

She shrieked and jumped away from me, narrowing those beautiful eyes. "Don't you dare, Professor Patton," she said, clicking her tongue and shaking her head. "You know I'm extra sensitive there."

My lips twisting into a smirk. "I could get it out of you in a different way."

Those eyes lit up with excitement that she quickly contained. She grabbed my hand and pulled me to the side of the hall as other students walked in for class today. She grabbed my hands, intertwined our fingers, and rocked back on her heels. "Would we be able to try ... you being harder on me?" she whispered. "Like, um, calling me mean names and maybe treating me like ..." She fumbled on her words, her cheeks growing redder by the moment.

"You want me to degrade you?" I asked.

"Maybe," she squeaked, hiding her face in my chest. "I mean, if you're not—"

"What would you like me to call you?"

She snapped her gaze up to mine. "You'll really do it?"

"I'll give you whatever kind of experience you'd like, but first, you have to answer me."

"Answer you?" she asked, furrowing her brow. "Y-you want me to tell you ..."

"What you'd like to be called."

"But I can't do that!" she exclaimed. "It's way too embarrassing."

Smirk widening, I pulled our hands up to my mouth and pressed my lips against her knuckles, eyes on her. "Then, I guess—"

"Slut," she whispered with the straightest face ever, and then she burst out into a fit of giggles. "And maybe a dirty ... a dirty whore." She pressed her thighs together, nipples hardening underneath her clothes. "Some other stuff too."

"Are you sure you want that?" I asked.

I remembered a few weeks ago, when she had asked me if I thought she was easy for taking Sex Education and I didn't want to break her down to tears like that ever again. But if she really wanted this, then I would oblige.

"Yes," she whispered, blushing. "I've been thinking about it for a while."

"Ask and you shall receive," I hummed, taking her hand and leading her into Radiant. After pulling off her coat, I handed it to the woman in the coatroom. "Do you want to try it out tonight? I can switch some classes around."

While she didn't say anything, her lips were curled into a small smile.

"We're going to have some ground rules," I started. "Okay?"

"Okay—"

Sierra stopped short, her gaze shifting behind me and her cheeks whitening. I glanced over my shoulder to see a guy about Sierra's age saunter into Radiant like he owned the place, the two top buttons on his shirt undone.

"I, um ..." Sierra said, swallowing. "Can we—"

"Look who it is," the guy taunted, spotting Sierra. "Thought you'd be here."

"Luke, what are you doing here?" she asked, making herself smaller behind me.

I shuffled in front of her and jutted out my hand. "Don't think we've met."

Luke hardened his glare at me, but placed his hand in mine. "Luke Carls, Sierra's ex."

"Steven Patton, Sierra's professor."

"Professor, huh?" Luke sneered.

After scooping up Sierra's hand, I leaned toward Luke. "I'd tell you to enjoy the night, but an immature brat like you won't be able to keep up with half the women here. But you can watch from the bar as I show your ex what being with a man is really like."

When I walked away, Sierra shuffled after me, glancing back and forth between me and Luke, who stood there, completely stunned, as if I would let him get off with attempting to belittle Sierra in front of me. If I didn't want to fuck Sierra in front of him just as a *fuck off* to him, I would've kicked him out.

"Degradation 101 tonight, Sierra," I said as we reached the classroom door. I clenched my jaw and didn't pay any attention to the fuming Luke still standing near the coatroom. "We're going to have a bit of a … field trip out into the main room tonight, if you don't mind."

Sierra opened and closed her mouth a handful of times. "I, um … are you sure?"

"If you'd feel more comfortable if I kicked him out, then I will," I reassured her.

"No. No, it's okay." A small smile crossed her face. "We can do that."

I moved closer to her and gently took her chin in my hand, lifting it so her focus was on me. "In today's class, I'm going to be mean to you. I'm going to say things to you that I don't really mean. Do things that might embarrass you. Call you names and degrade you. Okay?"

She nodded.

"And if I call you dumb"—I tucked some hair behind her ear—"I don't mean that you're stupid, but that you're mindless for me. My little plaything that I can use however I want. Understand?"

Again, she nodded.

"I need a verbal response, Miss Monroe."

"Yes, Sir."

I took her chin in my hand. "I need you to say your safeword if I hurt your feelings at all, if I do something or say something that you're not comfortable with."

She nodded. But I wanted her to really understand. Deeply.

"I refuse to let our class get in the way of …" I paused for a moment, getting ahead of myself. What really were we? A dominant and a submissive? Something more than that? I wasn't quite sure. All I really knew was that I cared about her.

More than I had cared about any other girl in the past.

"Of us?" she finished.

I stared at her for a couple of moments, then nodded. "Of us."

After another moment of silence, she finally tightened her grasp on my hand and nodded. "If I need my safeword, then I'll use it. I promise that I won't let it get in the way of"—her lips curled into a small smile—"us."

Good, because, tonight, I would show Luke Carls that Sierra was mine.

35

sierra

ONCE EVERYONE WAS SEATED in class for the night, Steven grabbed a black leather leash that could snap around my diamond necklace from a drawer and turned toward the class, his dark eyes on me. "Today's class is Degradation 101, and we'll be venturing into the amateur room tonight to practice."

Snapping the leash between his two strong hands, he curled his lips into a smirk that I had never seen before. Most of the time, Steven Patton had a friendly and lighthearted personality, but tonight, I had asked him to be mean to me.

And I couldn't wait.

"You will partner up and learn from the other doms and submissives in the main room," Steven said. "Do as they do. Respect your partner's safeword. And degrade each other like you never have before. Understand?"

With the heat gathering between my legs, I shifted in my seat and nodded with the class.

"Good," he started, walking toward the door. "Now, Sierra, why don't you lead us out?"

Heart racing and nipples aching, I stood.

"Remove your clothes, drop to your knees, and crawl."

"Crawl?" I repeated, sucking in a breath. "To where?"

"To me."

Once I pulled off my clothes so I stood naked in front of every-one, I dropped to my knees and crawled toward him. We had never done anything like this outside of the classroom, and I feared that I would do everything wrong with Luke watching. But Steven believed in me.

Or else he wouldn't make me do this, right?

Nerves zipped through me as my ass swayed side to side. Still, we had never been in the club as a couple. This would be the first time that he would officially show me off as his submissive—if I was; that part still wasn't clear—and I didn't want to fuck anything up. I wanted him to be proud of me.

Yet every time I moved closer to him, Steven took a step back.

"Crawl to me," he repeated again, continuing to shuffle back.

I followed him like a pet, my tits swaying against the floor and my cunt on display to my classmates.

When I finally reached the door where Steven stood, he cleared his throat. I stayed on my hands and knees and gazed up at him through my lashes. He buckled the leash around my diamond neck-lace and tightened his grip on me.

"You can be a good girl for once in your life," he spit. "Keep crawling. To the amateur room. Ass up. Back arched. I want everyone to see how much of a desperate, filthy whore you are for your master."

My pussy drooled at his words. I clenched and began crawling through the hallway and toward the amateur room. My heart raced as I passed through the bar area, where I spotted Luke hanging out, glaring at Steven, who walked me like a pet. Men who I had seen every now and then at Radiant looked our way, their eyes on me.

Steven stopped me once we reached a couch where Michelle, dressed in a black latex dominatrix outfit, played with a submissive. Steven wrapped his hand around the leash twice and pulled me toward him.

"Open that fucking mouth," he growled.

When I opened my mouth and stuck out my tongue, he spit on my face, then grabbed the wad of spit between his fingers and shoved it into my mouth. Four fingers deep, he pushed them deeper and deeper until I gagged on him.

Tears welled up in my eyes, but he didn't pull them out. He tucked his thumb underneath my chin to grab my jaw and let me gag, gargle, and choke on his fingers. I pulled back, but he kept them inside me until tears slid down my cheeks.

"Poor baby," he cooed. "Crying because you can't take a few fingers in your mouth."

More tears slid down my face from my burning eyes, but I sucked on his fingers as best as I could so I didn't disappoint him. But that wasn't the only reason. Luke was here and was watching.

And I wanted my revenge.

While I didn't have any feelings for him anymore, I wanted to show him what he was missing out on and the wild, raunchy girl I only became for Steven Patton—the BDSM-loving billionaire dom who, for some reason … liked me.

With his free hand, Steven tapped my cheek. "What'll happen when I shove my fat cock into that throat? Is my dumb little slut going to be able to take it? Or are you going to cry the entire time for me?"

I stared up at him through teary eyes, not backing down and refusing to pull away any more. I wanted his cock more than his fingers, and I would have to earn it. I had vowed to make him proud in the amateur room.

"It doesn't matter if those are crocodile tears or not. They give me so much power over you," he murmured. "They make you such a weak, desperate, fuckable mess of a woman that I can take advantage of."

Heat exploded through my core, and I nearly orgasmed on the spot from his words. I had known that he was dirty, but this dirty?! I hadn't thought I'd ever hear such degrading words leave his mouth. But I loved it. So much.

"Michelle," Steven said over the music, pulling up on the leash so I didn't sit back.

Leaning back on the armrest of the maroon leather couch, Michelle had her submissive on his knees and eating her cunt, her fingers laced in his thick blond hair. She gazed over at us through hazy eyes. "Look at you."

"Sierra wants to be a dirty whore tonight, and you know what dirty little whores get?" He gazed down at me and wiped my spit around my face again to make me a messy little slut for him. "Loads and loads and loads of cum."

After hopping off the armrest, Michelle took her submissive's chin in her hand and pulled him to a standing position, tugging him toward us. She stood behind him, her hand wrapped around his cock. "She's a dirty whore. You know how to take care of dirty whores, don't you? Fuck her mouth."

With his lips curled into a smirk, Steven pulled back on my leash once more so I sat on my heels. He grabbed my hair and tugged my head back so I stared up at them. Then, he rested his balls on my forehead and let his cock hang down across my face, just sitting there, jerking himself off.

"Open your fucking mouth," he growled. "Like the dirty little slut you are."

When I opened my mouth, Michelle's submissive pushed himself inside it.

"You're going to come for me," Michelle purred into her submissive's ear, her hand tightening around the base of his dick. "She's been a dirty whore, and dirty whores get all the cum they can suck out of a cock."

Warmth exploded through my pussy, and I thrust a hand between my legs to take care of myself. My fingers moved in circles around my clit, the pleasure pushing me higher and higher and higher into a state of mindlessness.

Instead of coming in my mouth, Michelle's submissive squirted his cum all over my face and onto Steven's cock. Steven dragged his palm all across my face to rub it into my skin and then pulled on my hair and shoved his cock into my throat from behind me.

"You're worthless," he said as he pounded into my throat, his hands in my hair and running across my neck quickly. "Good for nothing, except sucking on a cock and dumping balls' worth of cum inside your holes."

My throat squeaked, spit and drool running down my chin and onto my tits.

With his entire cock buried deep in my throat and his balls resting against my nose so I couldn't breathe, Steven stilled. "Swallow my cock like a desperate, filthy whore trying to make rent for the month."

I gripped one of his thighs with my free hand and continued rubbing my clit faster, the pressure rising quickly. I swallowed his cock over and over, making it harder to breathe, and then my pussy exploded with pleasure. I screamed out on his cock, my entire body shaking.

"Is that all it takes for you to come?" He chuckled menacingly. "Fuck my slut's dirty mouth? You're so easy." When he pulled his cock out of me, he dragged it around my face. "So easy to ruin."

He pulled me to my feet and bent me over the couch. Before I knew it, he plunged himself deep inside my pussy from behind, tugged both hands behind my back, and began thrusting wildly.

Incoherent moans tumbled out of my mouth. I threw my head back, brow furrowed.

Holy shit. Holy shit. Holy shit.

Michelle giggled and pulled lipstick from her purse, handing it to Steven.

Steven grabbed the stick and uncapped it with his mouth, spitting the cap out onto the couch and releasing one of my hands. "Ruin yourself with it."

As he pounded into me, I took the lipstick in a shaky hand and placed it against my chest, writing the words *dirty, filthy, whore, Steven's slut,* and more all over in crooked letters. All for my master.

"What are you?"

"I'm a dirty whore," I cried.

"Keep repeating it while I fuck you," he growled, seizing my hips and slamming into me repeatedly before I could even get my bearings. "We need to get it through that empty head of yours that you're a good-for-nothing slut."

"I'm a dirty whore," I cried. "I'm a dirty whore."

He grabbed me by the hair, pulled my back to his chest, and slapped me across the face. "Louder, so everyone can hear you. They're watching to see how dirty, how filthy, how desperate you really are."

"I'm a dirty whore! I'm a dirty whore! I'm a dirty whore!" I repeated between thrusts.

"You've found yourself a fan club," Steven growled into my ear, gesturing around the club to a bunch of couples and men sitting at the bar, watching Steven fuck me completely senseless. "I'd bet they'd agree that you're a filthy, whore who loves being full of cock, huh?"

"I'm a dirty whore," I repeated, pressure building higher and higher. "I love being full of cock! Please fill up my pussy and breed me, Sir! Please make me your filthy little cumbucket, so I can fulfill my duties to—"

Steven slammed himself into me and grunted loudly behind me. I curled my toes and screamed out in pleasure as an orgasm ripped through my entire body. My legs shook so wildly that they gave out, and I collapsed onto the couch, next to Michelle, breathing heavily and completely satisfied.

"So I can fulfill my duties to you, Sir," I said breathlessly.

36

AFTER STEPPING INTO THE TUB, I collapsed in Steven's arms, completely exhausted from Radiant. I sank down in the water and blew some bubbles with my exhale, shoulders rolling forward and stress leaving my body from the temperature.

"How're you feeling?" Steven asked, gently rubbing my thigh from behind, the water shifting as he did so.

"Okay," I whispered.

Candles crackled around us.

"Are you sure?"

"Yes."

"Even with your ex ..."

I giggled. "I can't believe you said that to him."

When Luke had walked into Radiant, I'd almost shit myself right there on the spot. I thought Luke would flip Steven off, not shake his hand and try to belittle me in front of him. And Steven?! Possessive Steven?! Warmth gushed between my thighs. I loved that side of him.

Loved with a capital L.

"What did you expect me to say to him?" he hummed. "He'd made you feel like shit."

"Where did that even come from?" I said, grasping my belly in a fit of chuckles.

"Where did what come from?"

After lowering my voice to replicate his, I said, " 'I'd tell you to enjoy the night, but an immature brat like you won't be able to keep up with half the women here.' " I leaned back against him, shoulders jolting back and forth. "Steven, that was golden."

He chuckled. "Listen, if Michelle got her hands on him, he would be screaming his safeword within a minute and attempting to crawl out the back door."

I wiped happy tears from my cheeks, picturing Michelle crushing Luke's tiny balls with her pointed heel, him screaming in pain and limping toward the door as she chased after him with that mischievous grin she always had.

"He was looking for trouble when he walked into my club, and he found it."

Another chuckle escaped my mouth. "My big, bad Steven Patton."

I should've been more serious because Luke had been the bane of my existence for so long, but it had been so refreshing to see someone who wasn't Heather stick up for me. And to see Steven this annoyed at a man he barely knew because of me …

Someone knocked on the door.

"Mr. Patton?" a woman said.

All the silliness seemed to evaporate from my body, and I stiffened. *Who is this?*

"Yes, Brigitta?"

"Mr. Thornton would like to know if you'd like anything before we leave."

Maybe she was his staff. But this late at night?

Steven paused and glanced down at me. "Are you hungry?"

"A bit."

"What would you like?"

I glanced over my shoulder and up at him. "Do you have smoothies?"

"Two smoothies," Steven called to Brigitta.

"Yes, Mr. Patton."

Thank goodness that she hadn't called him sir, or I might've had a breakdown.

"Who's Brigitta?" I asked, jealousy nipping at my insides.

"Thornton is my chef, and Brigitta cleans when I'm working. She must have stayed later tonight," he said, wrapping his arms around my waist and pulling me closer to his strong chest. He lowered his voice and chuckled. "They think that I don't know they're dating."

"They're dating?!" I exclaimed. "That's so cute."

"They've worked for me for ten years now, and the number of times I've caught them staring at each other ..." He smiled softly to himself, his breath warm on my neck. "It almost makes me believe in love."

"You don't believe in love?" I whispered.

He stiffened behind me. "Do you?"

"I do."

A long pause.

"What does it feel like?" he finally asked.

"A lot of people think love is being happy all the time with someone else, like a never-ending honeymoon phase," I said, voice quieting. "But that's not what love is to me. Love is being safe with someone, staying through the hard times, and wanting what's best for them even if it hurts you in the end."

Another long pause.

"Have you ever been in love before?" he said behind me.

"I've loved my family, but as for another person ..." I swallowed hard and pressed my hand against my inner thigh under the bubbles because I didn't want him to see how much I wanted to scream out, *Yes!* "I'm not sure. Have you?"

"No."

A single word from his mouth squeezed at my heart.

"Oh."

He stiffened even harder, a bunch of *ums* and *uhs* tumbling out of his mouth. "I mean—"

"Mr. Patton, should I bring them in?" Brigitta asked.

Silence washed over us once more, and I settled back against him, deciding to let it go.

"Can she bring them in?" Steven asked me.

"Steven"—I stifled a small laugh—"everyone has already seen me naked."

"At Radiant," he clarified. "And just because people have seen you naked once doesn't give anyone the right to see you naked again or in any other circumstance. That's how consent works, love. Tell me you understand that."

I paused for a moment. "I never really thought of it that way."

While I hadn't done anything serious with Luke, I'd always felt like he expected me to do certain things or act a certain way just because I had done it before. But sometimes, I didn't feel like it. Sometimes, I'd wanted to just be without having to offer my body up for him.

"I understand now," I whispered.

He curled his lips into a small smile and pushed some wet hair off my forehead. "So?"

"She can come in," I said. "It's okay."

Steven laid one arm over my nipples, which were peeking out just above the bubbles, as if to still provide me with some decency. "Brigitta, you can come in."

The door opened, and a petite woman shuffled into the room with a wooden serving tray. She set it on the sink counter and grabbed both glasses filled to the top with, what looked to be, strawberry-mango smoothies. She handed me one.

"Thank you, Brigitta."

She nodded and handed one to Steven. "Of course, Miss Monroe."

"You can call me Sierra."

"Well then, enjoy your bath, Sierra and Mr. Patton," she said, shuffling to the door.

I smiled and sank down even more, excited to finally spend the holidays with someone who was just as lonely as I was, who didn't have a family and wanted to spend time with me as much as I wanted to spend with them.

The holidays couldn't come soon enough. While I couldn't spend thousands or even hundreds of dollars on him for a gift, I had—what I think was—the best present for him that I had ever picked out for anyone. And I couldn't wait to see his face on Christmas morning.

37

steven

"YOU'RE HERE EARLY," Sierra said, glancing up from the stack of wrapped gifts on her bed. Halfway through shoving them into a large red sack, she stopped and smiled, her dark hair pulled back into a high ponytail. "Did Heather let you in?"

"No," I said, sliding my hands into the pockets of my suit pants and leaning against her doorframe, my chest lighter than it usually was this time of year. "I got in good with the security guard up front."

She burst out into a fit of laughter, her cheeks rounding. A warm feeling spread through my chest as I watched her giggle at my little joke because we both knew that the security guard up front would *never* let me in without her. He hated my guts.

"Thanks for letting him in, Heather!" she said, glancing behind me.

I looked over my shoulder to see Hector's submissive smirking wickedly at Sierra. "Have a good Christmas Eve. I'll see you both tomorrow night for dinner. Hector invited me to come over to your place, Mr. Professor Man."

"Heather," Sierra scolded quietly, cheeks turning red.

"Mr. Professor Man?" I repeated, arching a brow at Sierra.

"That's our nickname for you," Heather said.

"Heather!" Sierra exclaimed. "You don't have to tell him."

My lips curled into a smile, and I hummed, "Is that so, Miss Monroe?"

After Heather giggled behind me, she padded down the hallway, and the apartment door closed. Sierra shyly bit back a smile and continued stuffing her bag with many small gifts.

"I'm Mr. Professor Man to you?" I asked, brow arched.

But my stomach twisted. It sounded like a play name, like a nickname for someone Sierra was just hooking up with. And I wondered if that was what she thought about me—someone just good enough to hook up with a few times until she found someone else.

"No, that's who you are to my friends," Sierra said, tying the bag. She walked over to me and wrapped her arms around my waist, her chin on the center of my chest as she looked up at me. "You're Sir to me."

I hardened against her stomach and captured her jaw in my hand. "Am I?"

"Mmhmm."

"Does that mean you aren't going to be bratty for me tonight?" I said, drawing my thumb across her lower lip and then sinking it into her mouth, letting her suck on it. "Do I get to do anything I want with you?"

"Maybe."

"Maybe?"

"Depends on what it is," she said.

"Our first private lesson," I said, watching how she drew her tongue around my knuckle. I pressed myself harder against her, loving how submissive she was for me even if she wanted to act like she wasn't. "Just for you."

She leaned her upper body back slightly, staring up at me through wide and playful eyes. "What are you going to teach me tonight, Professor?" A sly smirk crossed her face. "It'd better be something good."

"Are you suggesting that it's never *not* good?" I said, stepping toward her.

She shuffled back a couple of feet, legs hitting the bed.

"Because I seem to remember you crying from how good it was last time."

"Hmm." She beamed, placing a finger on her lips. "I can't seem to remember."

"Maybe I need to help you," I offered, biting back a grin from all the sinister things I wanted to do to Sierra that I knew she wasn't ready for. "Do you want me to wrap my belt around your throat to use as a leash and walk you up and down your dorm—"

"No!" she exclaimed, waving her arms back and forth. "I remember. I remember!"

A low chuckle escaped my throat, and she hurried to the sack.

"What's in the sack?" I asked.

When she tossed it over her shoulder, I arched my brow and grabbed it from her. She wasn't hauling this all the way back to my car by herself. She thanked me and grabbed her backpack, filled with her overnight belongings.

"It's just some … things."

"Things?"

"Presents." She smirked. "And not presents for you."

"Woooow," I drew out playfully.

She giggled. "Don't worry. I have something better for you."

Warmth exploded through my chest. *God, I love her smile.*

Honestly, she didn't have to get me anything for Christmas. I had been so fucking excited since last class to be able to take her home tonight, have her stay with me all week, wake up next to her day after day …

"We have a dinner reservation at seven," I said. "We should get going."

"A dinner reservation?" she asked, scoffing. "How boring."

"Boring? What would you rather do?"

Another breathtaking grin crossed her face. "Let's order a pizza, make hot cocoa, and watch Christmas movies tonight! We can go out to dinner any night of the week, but Christmas Eve is only once a year. A new tradition!"

"A tradition, huh?"

A tradition that happened every year? That meant that she expected we'd be together next year, and the year after, and possibly the year after that too. And while I had spent the past thirty years of my life with the Pattons—the husband and wife who had adopted all of us and now passed—I had never had anything stable with anyone but them. Now that they were both gone, my life had turned into an unstable mess once more.

But Sierra was proposing something long-term without even knowing it.

"Earth to Steven," Sierra said, bouncing on her toes in front of me. "So?"

"Let's do it."

Her eyes widened to the size of saucers. "Really?"

"Anything for you, *love.*"

After throwing her arms around my shoulders, she jumped into my arms and pulled me down into a tight hug, that sparkle in her eye and the excitement in her voice making me smile. Making me ... *happy.*

An emotion that I feared.

Because happiness could be ripped away in a millisecond.

I grabbed her hand and guided her to the door. "Let's start a tradition."

38

sierra

"ENOUGH MOVIES," Steven said after a Christmas movie marathon and tons of pizza. He turned off the living room television, cleared his throat, and walked to the door. "Wait here, love, and undress for me. I have a surprise for you."

My eyes widened. "A surprise?"

His chuckle echoed down the hallway. "You'd best be undressed by the time I return."

After sucking in a breath, I hopped up from the couch and tugged off my clothes, lingering in just my underwear near the floor-to-ceiling windows. Steven had mentioned that we would have a private lesson tonight.

When Steven returned, he held a metal bar and festive tinsel in his hands. His gaze dropped to my body, and he arched a brow as he placed the bar on the coffee table. "I thought I said to undress."

"I am undressed."

"All of it, love."

I glanced toward the open windows, where anyone could look in and see us.

"Here?" I whispered. "In front of the windows? Don't you have a BDSM room?"

He chuckled. "One, why are you afraid of some windows? I've fucked you in front of members of Radiant before, and we're too many stories up in the air for anyone to see you. And two, I have no reason to have a BDSM room in my home. I don't bring anyone home."

Except me.

Warmth exploded through my body. Steven had kept all his relationships before me solely at Radiant? He hadn't brought any other woman home the way that he brought me home? Hadn't shared his bedroom with them either, I supposed.

"But if you'd prefer I shut the blinds, then I will."

A giddy giggle left my mouth, and I shook my head. "Here is fine."

"Are you sure?"

I dropped my gaze to the rope of tinsel he had lying across his palm and the metal bar on the coffee table, then nodded. Warmth gushed through my pussy, and I pressed my thighs together. "Yes."

His lips curled into that infamous smirk he had flashed me the day I met him by the bar. My nipples tightened, my breath catching in my throat. God, I couldn't wait for this. He had teased me with the mention of tying me up so many times now.

"Knees," he ordered, his calming voice replaced with the one he used at Radiant.

After dropping to my knees in front of him, I stared up at him through my lashes.

He captured my chin in his hand and drew his thumb across my lips. "Good girl."

With the tinsel, Steven tied my wrists together, then created intricate knots up my forearms to bind them together too. From this position and the knots, my tits pressed together, and I could barely move my upper body.

"Get into doggy—elbows on the carpet, ass in the air," he ordered.

Once I maneuvered myself to a doggy position, just as he'd asked, I looked back at him to catch him checking out my ass. He smirked and grabbed the metal bar from the coffee table, then dropped to his knees behind me.

"This is called a spreader," he said, locking it around one of my knees. He gently tapped the other one so I would move my legs further apart. Once my legs were spread far enough apart, he locked it around my opposite leg. "It keeps your legs spread, no matter how much you want to pull them together. Understand?"

I nodded.

He dropped his hand between my thighs and gently massaged my sopping pussy. My first instinct was to pull my legs together to ease the ache, but I couldn't move my arms or my legs, leaving me completely vulnerable to him.

"Welcome to your private lesson, Miss Monroe. Bondage 101."

In doggy—with my ass in the air, my legs spread with a bar, and forearms bound together—I tugged on the restraints as he toyed with my pussy, his fingers moving in and out of me, his thumb gliding against my swollen clit.

I whined, "Sir ..."

A satisfied grunt escaped his mouth, and he stood in front of the windows behind me, pulling off his shirt and undoing his pants. I nearly drooled, staring at him and impatiently waiting for him to fuck me senseless.

"Patience, love."

"Please, Sir. I need it."

"I could leave you here all night and not fuck you if I wanted to," he hummed. "Be good."

"I am good."

"Good girls do as their masters say," he murmured. "And I told you to be patient."

After whining again, I wiggled my ass back and forth in an attempt to grind my thighs against my pussy. I needed something— anything—to ease the ache between my legs, to make me feel good. He couldn't just leave me like this.

He walked to the hallway and disappeared, saying nothing more.

"Steven!" I cried. "Please! I'll be patient. I'll be your good girl. I promise!"

A moment passed, and I whined again, my pussy right in front of the windows, showing myself off to everyone who wanted to watch. It was drooling, the wetness dripping down my pussy lips and onto my thighs.

"Sir, please," I whined. "I'm a good girl."

Steven sauntered back into the room with a wedge pillow and leather cuffs. Moonlight flooded in through the windows, bouncing off his muscular body and making him look like a god. I attempted to grind my thighs together once more, my pussy pulsing wildly.

He placed the pillow on the ground beside me, then pushed it underneath my body so my hips were supported by the cushion. Then, he dropped down behind me once more. "You attempting to grind your thighs together when I told you to be patient doesn't scream good girl to me, Sierra."

"I'm sorry, Sir. I—"

When he pressed the head of his cock against my wet pussy, I whimpered. He pushed his cock back and forth over my entrance, teasing and taunting me with it, gliding it across my clit in small, torturous circles. I arched my back and attempted to push back, but I couldn't move.

"I'm in control, Sierra," he said, peppering kisses up my bare back. "I can do anything that I want to this pretty little body." His mouth lingered when he reached the back of my neck. "And you can't do anything about it. You're mine for tonight. All mine."

And with that, he slammed into my tight cunt. I moaned out in pleasure, eyes rolling back into my head as he seized my hips and used my body however he pleased, like he'd promised me that he would. Over and over, he thrust into me until my cunt was dripping all over his pillow.

"You're mine," he growled against my shoulder, gently gnawing on the skin. "All mine."

After thrusting into me for the next five minutes—slow, then fast, then slow, then fast—he took the wedge pillow away from me and helped me to a standing position. My forearms were still bound together, my legs spread from the bar between my knees. Juices dripped from my pussy down both thighs.

While the tinsel was still wrapped around my wrists, he grabbed leather cuffs and snapped them around my wrists and gazed up at the ceiling toward the smoke alarm. I furrowed my brow as he reached for it.

What … what was he going to do with the smoke alarm?!

Another whine left my mouth. All I wanted was for him to slip inside me. Pound into me. Over and over and over until my pussy was crying on his big, fat cock. Until he was … coming inside me and refusing to pull out.

A shiver ran through my body, more juices running down my thigh.

Fuck, this isn't a thought that should turn me on.

But having my professor's cum buried deep inside me … having my professor *breed* me …

Steven reached up and pulled the smoke alarm right off the ceiling, revealing a hook underneath it. I furrowed my brow harder, confused as to why there was a hook on the ceiling in a skyrise as nice as his. Couldn't he have that replaced?

But when he grabbed the cuffs snapped around my hands, I widened my eyes.

"Oh no," I said. "No, no, no, no, no, no, no. You … you can't hang me from the ceiling!"

"I'll do as I please with you."

I pulled my wrists away from him. "But I'll break the ceiling if you—"

"Sierra," he said sternly, "are you disobeying me?"

"No, but—"

"I was going to save punishment for another class, but if you want to be a little brat tonight, then I will teach you how to follow orders," he growled, his gaze dark and stern. "I'll give you one last chance to present your wrists to me."

Heart racing, I stared between him and the hook, then moved my wrists toward him.

My heart pounded inside my chest, and I ran my tongue across my lip as he hooked my cuffs to the ceiling, lifting me in the air. My toes barely touched the ground as I hung there helplessly for him to torture tonight.

"My little plaything," he hummed, grabbing more tinsel from the coffee table. He wrapped one end around my throat, pulled up the spreader so my knees were nearly against my chest, and tied the other side to the bar. "I'll save your punishment for another day."

I hung in the air, legs spread, pussy dripping with anticipation, and eyes on him. He held my gaze with his dark one and placed his hands on my thighs, stepping between my legs and pressing his cock against my entrance.

"Beg for it."

"Steven …"

"Beg. For. It."

"Please!" I cried.

"I don't believe you want it that badly," he murmured, teasing me with his dick.

"Please, Sir, give me your huge—"

Before I could finish my sentence, he slammed his cock into me, as deep as he could get it. I threw my head back and came almost instantly, legs shaking and eyes rolling back into my head.

"That's my good girl," he praised. "Come undone for me."

With my body trembling in his hands, he held me still and pulled out so just his head was inside my pulsing pussy. Then, he slammed into me again. Deep. I threw my head back and cried out in pleasure, another rush exploding through me.

"Did you just come again?" he asked, a low chuckle escaping his mouth.

"S-S-Steven …"

"Answer me, love."

"Yes," I whimpered. "P-p-please."

A satisfied grunt escaped his lips, and he thrust into me. Pleasure rushed through my body as I hung helplessly from the ceiling and in his arms. He groped my ass with his large hands, pulling my cheeks apart and using me to thrust deeper and deeper and deeper.

"I'm going to bury my cum so deep inside you," he growled against my lips.

I nodded desperately. "Please," I breathed out, kissing him on the mouth. "Breed me."

As if something took control of him as soon as the words left my mouth, he began pounding into me wildly, his eyes rolling back and his tongue swiping across my lower lip, his hands all over my body. While his thrusts were fast and savage, he didn't pull his cock all the way out of me once.

He slammed himself into me over and over again, at least three inches of himself in me at all times, as if he wanted to make sure every drop of his cum made it inside my tight, wet, desperate pussy.

"Please, Sir! Give me your c-c-cum!" I cried as we came at the same exact time.

39

steven

AS I LOOSENED the rope around Sierra's forearms, she gazed up at me, her cheeks flushed and that diamond necklace glimmering under the light. She reached up and fiddled with it around her neck, a small smile on her face.

"Did that satisfy all those little urges in you?" I asked, loving the way she had asked me to breed her.

After I freed her, she sat down and leaned back on her hands. "What do you mean?"

I grabbed my suit jacket from off the couch and slung it around her shoulders to cover her body. Nobody was in the room, and the door was closed, but I still wanted to give her some decency.

"Do you remember the first night of class, when you told me that you watched BDSM porn?" A low chuckle escaped my throat when her eyes widened in horrific embarrassment. "You also mentioned bondage."

"I-I did?!" she exclaimed, dropping her gaze to her feet and giggling. "Oh God."

I gently took her chin between my fingers and lifted. "Did it meet your expectations?"

She thought about it for a moment, and then her lips curled into a smile. "Maybe."

"Maybe?"

And then she wrapped her arms around my torso and hugged me. I stiffened because while we had been intimate before in the bathtub, nothing compared to this.

It seemed like she felt safe and secure in my arms, in my classroom, and as my sub.

No matter how far I pushed her, no matter how close to her boundaries I came, she knew that I would protect her at all costs. That I wouldn't let anything happen to her even if she had no control.

"Thank you," she whispered, placing her head on the center of my chest. "It was amazing."

Before she could pull away, I wrapped my arms around her body and relaxed. "Of course, love," I murmured, leading Sierra to the bedroom.

She fell asleep quickly and with ease, but I stayed up, staring at the ceiling.

Unable to sleep.

So, I slipped into my home office and unlocked my desk drawer. After pulling out a stack of papers, I set them on the desk and stared down at the BDSM contract that I'd had a lawyer draft between us.

Heart racing, I sat down and read through it three more times. I had never offered anybody a contract like this before. Hell, I had never even *thought* about offering any woman a contract like this.

But what if she didn't want it? What if she would rather keep things the way they were? What if I gave her this contract tomorrow and she rejected it, laughed in my face, and told me that nobody would ever sign anything like this from me? Like so many foster families had told me that I wasn't good enough, that nobody would want me.

After squeezing my eyes closed, I forced out a breath. Sierra wouldn't do that, but it still worried me because there was always a chance for anything to happen. If I didn't allow myself to be vulner-able, then I couldn't be hurt.

A knock came at my door, and I snapped my gaze up to see Thornton.

"I thought you left hours ago," I said.

"Finishing preparations for tomorrow's dinner," he said, glancing over his shoulder and toward the living room, a low chuckle escaping his mouth. "And Brigitta stayed behind to deep-clean the kitchen after I greased it up."

Why couldn't I enjoy love like that? Why couldn't it be as easy for me as it was for them? I had been dirt poor, traded from family to family to family, and now, I was worth a billion dollars. I'd thought money would change everything. But still, I always felt the same—terrified to be happy.

"Enjoy your night with Brigitta. She's a lucky girl."

"So is Sierra." Thornton paused. "I haven't seen you this excited for Christmas in years."

A low chuckle escaped my throat. "Do these stress lines make me look excited?"

He glanced down at the contract on my desk. "I think you're stressing yourself out because when you're with Sierra ..." He paused for a moment, his lips curling into a small smile. "You look like you're at peace."

At peace? Is that what Sierra does to me? Am I really the one who stressed myself out?

"Merry Christmas," Thornton said, pushing himself off the door. "And, Mr. Patton ..."

"Yes?"

"You deserve to be happy."

With that, he disappeared into the hallway, his footsteps leading away from my office. I stared at the empty doorway and frowned. *Do I really deserve to be happy? After all these years, after all the families who returned me, am I worth it?*

Worthy of happiness? Worthy of love?

After rubbing my forefinger and thumb against my forehead, I reopened my desk drawer and picked out the matte-black gift box that I had bought before I picked up Sierra earlier from her dorm. I set the contract inside, nerves gnawing at my insides, and closed it before I had the chance to stop myself.

"Steven!" Sierra called from the bedroom, her voice groggy, as if she had just woken up.

And I hoped to God—a God that I didn't even believe in—that she hadn't heard my conversation with Thornton a few moments ago.

"Come cuddle."

"I'll be there in a second, Sierra," I said, walking to the door and glancing down the hallway at the door open ajar, just how I had left it. I walked with the black box to the living room and set the box underneath the sparkling Christmas tree.

Honestly, I didn't know if I believed that I was worthy of anything. I didn't know if I would even have the courage to give this to her tomorrow. But I hoped that I did. Because I wanted to be happy. I wanted it so badly.

"Steven," she murmured from the bedroom again.

I walked down the hallway and slipped into the room with her, my heart swelling at the sight of her in my bed, her hair a mess of frizz and curls against the pillows and the moonlight flooding in through the floor-to-ceiling windows, making her pale skin glimmer.

"Come to bed," she mumbled, eyes half open.

Once I pulled my shirt over my head, I crawled up into bed with her, curled my arm around her waist, and cuddled her from behind. She moved against me to get comfortable and snuggled into the pillow. I sank my nose into her hair and closed my eyes.

Maybe Thornton was right. Sierra was my peace.

And I might even love her.

40

steven

"MERRY CHRISTMAS!" Sierra beamed at me, her head on the center of my chest and her fingers strumming across my naked abdomen. She was wide awake, which meant that she must've been up for at least a while now.

"Morning," I mumbled, my stomach twisting. "Merry Christmas."

"I'm so excited for today," she said, lifting her head off me and resting it on her pillow.

While I had been excited last night, this morning ... I didn't feel good. I had twisted and turned in bed all night until very early this morning and could barely swallow the bile heavy in my throat. All I could think about last night was ... how she'd react to my present.

Thornton had said that I deserved to be happy, but did I really? And if I did, what would it even feel like? Would I always fear that it'd be ripped right out from underneath my fingers for the rest of my life? Would I always fear that this was all an act, that Sierra would never truly care for me?

"Do you wanna make hot cocoa with me and open gifts?"

"Sure," I whispered, wiping the sleep from my eyes.

"Wait!" Sierra exclaimed, jumping up naked and rummaging through her bag. "Before we go out to open gifts …" She tugged out a wrapped box and handed it to me. "Technically, I was supposed to give you this last night, but I fell asleep after your *present* to me."

Sitting on the edge of the bed with a thin sheet over my lap, I arched my brow and ripped off the blue wrapping paper to see two pairs of matching red-and-black holiday-themed pajama pants and black shirts.

She hopped onto the bed next to me and grinned. "It was a tradition in my family to dress in the same pajamas on Christmas Eve." She glanced away and blushed, kicking her legs back and forth. "We don't have to do it, but …"

"Love," I murmured, tucking some hair behind her ear, "I'd love to match with you."

She gazed at me through wide eyes filled with excitement. "Really?"

I slipped out of bed and pulled on the fluffy pants, wishing that I had a tradition to share with her, too, but I had never celebrated the holidays like she had. More nerves bubbled up in my belly. Hopefully, we could do this again next year too.

But maybe she'd be onto bigger and better things, new opportunities, other men.

I winced at the thought. *Fuck, that hurt.*

Once we made hot cocoa and began opening the small gifts we had gotten each other, I leaned against the couch near the gift I'd boxed yesterday. All week long, I had been looking forward to today, but now that we sat in front of the tree, unwrapping gifts, my stomach gurgled, my muscles were tight, and I was thinking the worst.

The matte-black box that I had placed underneath the tree seemed to glare at me, taunt me. And while it couldn't talk—because it was an inanimate fucking object—all I could hear was that I wasn't good enough for her. That she would never see me the way I saw her.

That all of this was somehow a lie.

All the late nights. All the early mornings. Waking up next to her with my nose buried in her hair. Breathing in her shampoo. Seeing her smile. Those lips. The brightness in her eyes. Caring for her in the tub with all the bubbles.

I feared that it was all a lie. Because nobody gave a shit about me.

Ever.

"Here," Sierra said, grabbing a small box. "This is *one of* my last gifts to you."

I grabbed the box from her and unwrapped it, pulling out a gift card to Giant Eagle and arching my brow. "Love, did you buy a gift for yourself?"

"No, of course not!" she said in a fit of giggles. "I bought it so *you* have an excuse to go grocery shopping with me."

She had bought this just for me to spend time with her. *Fuck.*

Her cheeks rounded. "Plus, you haven't even seen the entire store yet."

The more time I spent with her, the harder and harder I fell. And the harder the pain would be when she left me once she discovered that I wasn't really good for her, that there were far better men out there worthy of her time, that I was just some broken man who was both so desperate for love and scared of commitment.

After thanking her, I walked over to the tree. I had two last gifts for her, one near the couch and one behind some of Michelle's and Hector's gifts. I stared down at them, my heart pounding so loudly that it deafened me.

My fingers trembled as I leaned down, the terror lodged in my throat, making it harder and harder to breathe. I cursed at myself as I bent at the hip to grab the smaller box, my leg lifting off the ground slightly and kicking the gift with the contract underneath the couch.

Fuck.

The moment I kicked it so she wouldn't see or ask about it, guilt, sadness, hurt, and even more shame rushed through every fiber of my being. I couldn't do it. I couldn't even fucking ask her.

I could've turned back. I could've reached underneath the couch to pick it up.

But my fears had me in a fucking choke hold.

"Here's one more," I said, handing her a diamond tennis bracelet that matched her necklace, my words less tense but my body full of anxiety. I stared underneath the couch as she opened her present, feeling so stupid.

She tore off the wrapping paper and opened up the small box, her lips curling into a frown. "Steven, this is too much. I thought we decided on something small and thoughtful." She paused, drawing her fingers across the diamonds. "But it's beautiful."

"I'm glad you like it," I forced out, unable to look her in the eye.

Why was I such a fuckup when it came to relationships? First, I couldn't tell her what the damn necklace meant. She'd had to hear it from my own sister. And now, I couldn't even ask her to be my submissive even though that was what she'd technically been for weeks.

After setting the box on the ground beside her, Sierra hopped up, grabbed my hand, and eyed the red sack of gifts that she had been putting together last night when I picked her up. "I have something else for you, but we have to go somewhere."

"Where are you taking me?" I asked.

"It's a surprise."

41

steven

"ARE YOU SURE WE HAVE TIME?" Sierra asked, walking down the sidewalk next to me.

I stopped at the crosswalk with her and zippered up her jacket all the way. "Yes, love."

"Dinner doesn't start until six?"

She was full of questions this morning, wasn't she? And I still didn't know where she was taking me with this sack full of presents that I had draped over my shoulder. We had been walking for ten minutes in the cold.

"Right," I said. "Dinner doesn't start for another five hours."

"Good," she said. "Because I don't know how long we'll be here."

We continued up another block of the Pittsburgh streets in the frigid winter air.

I tightened my grasp on the red sack and arched my brow at her. "Would you like to tell me where we're going?" I asked. "We could've taken my car."

"It's one of your gifts," she said, chewing on her inner cheek and stopping on the side of the road. She glanced across the street at a building, then pulled me toward it when we were allowed to cross.

"I hope you don't mind," she said, "but I promised the kids at my work that I'd come visit them today. They're all either waiting for adoption or between foster homes right now, and they don't really have anyone else besides the adults who work here."

As soon as Sierra pushed the door open, I listened to footsteps padding down the hall.

"Miss Sierra!" a little girl with blonde pigtails yelled, running up to us. She wrapped both small arms around Sierra's knee and stared up at her with a big, toothless grin, her chin on Sierra's thigh. "You actually came!"

My smile dropped, uneasy feelings rushing through me at her words. She—and the rest of the kids—had wished that Sierra would come, but they had been let down so many times that they didn't believe that she actually would.

God, I knew that feeling too well.

"Of course I came," she said, twirling her fingers around the child's pigtails. "I promised."

The girl turned to me and pointed. "Did you bring your family?"

Sierra glanced over at me, gave me a soft smile, then crouched down to be at the girl's level. "Something like that. He's my helper. Sorta like Santa's helper but a lot cooler." She giggled and nodded to the bag. "See, he brought all the gifts."

The little girl's pupils grew even wider as she stared at the sack. A couple of other young children jogged up to Sierra, wrapping her up in big hugs. She whispered something quiet to the kids, and they all looked at me.

And then, in a moment, ten of them ran over, grabbing my hands and pulling me toward a back room. A fit of, "Come on," and, "Let's go," escaping their mouths.

I stumbled along, peering over my shoulder at Sierra, who smiled and picked up the girl with pigtails to follow us.

"Where are they taking me?" I asked.

"To the multipurpose room," she said.

We walked down a hallway that was covered with paintings of Christmas trees, Hanukkah menorahs, and snow falling from the sky, then into a large room, filled with easels and toys as well as all types of holiday decor.

"This month, we've been learning about all our different cultures and the holidays that we celebrate," Sierra said, crouching down in front of a couple of the children once they released their hold on me. "And for the past couple of days, they've been preparing for Christmas for those of us who celebrate."

My lips curled into a small smile as I leaned against the door, a lightness in my chest as I looked at Sierra. "Well, you've done a great job. The drawings hanging up on the walls are brilliant. Some of the best I've seen."

"We heard that Sierra and you celebrate Christmas too!" the girl from earlier exclaimed.

I nodded. "We celebrated this morning."

"Well," Sierra said, glancing at the kids, "who wants to do it?"

"Me!" a handful of kids shouted at the same time, hands shooting up.

"Do what?" I asked, brow arched as the kids disappeared behind a wall.

A moment later, they reappeared with a large holiday gift bag in their small hands, all of them working together to hold it up. They walked over to me and lifted it into the air for me to grab. Confused, I took the bag from them and looked at Sierra.

"What's this?" I asked.

"It's a gift for you," she said. "The kids made it."

Warmth exploded through my chest, my gaze flickering from the bag to the children giddily jumping up and down, waiting in anticipation. I opened and closed my mouth a handful of times, my words suddenly lodged in my throat.

"F-for me?" I asked.

"Yeah!" all the kids shouted.

After swallowing hard, I crouched to their level and set the bag on the ground. I pulled out some tissue paper and gazed inside at all the small canvases, covered in globs of paint.

I took the first one out, and a small boy raised his hand and leaned forward. "That one is mine!"

"Wow," I breathed out, a smile on my face. "I love it."

"Do you know what it is?" He beamed.

"What?"

He pointed to two large figures in the center. "That's you and Miss Sierra." Then, he gestured to all the smaller stick figures next to us. "And that's us! Miss Sierra said that you both don't celebrate Christmas with anyone, so I wanted to draw us as one big, happy family."

Tears welled up in my eyes, and I stared down at the painting, attempting not to cry in front of all these kids and in front of Sierra. I continued to pull out more and more canvases, each similar to the first, but us cooking or playing in a pool, at the beach or having a party.

After I pulled out the last canvas, I wiped tears from my eyes and glanced up at Sierra, who held the girl with pigtails in her lap. She rested her head against the girl's but stared at me with a soft smile.

"Why don't you open your gifts?" she said, nudging the girl toward the sack of gifts that the other kids were getting into.

And when the girl ran off, Sierra walked over to me slowly, fiddling with her dress.

"Come here," I murmured, taking her hand and drawing her closer to me. "Why'd you bring me here?"

"If you don't want to stay, I can meet you back at your place before six," she said.

I drew my thumb across her cheek. "Why'd you bring me here?"

"Because ..." She shrugged and peered down at her shoes shyly. "I wanted you to experience what Christmas with a family feels like. Even though they're not related to you, I thought—"

Before she could finish her sentence, I pulled her closer and pressed my lips to hers.

She sucked in a surprised breath. And then she placed her hands on my chest, her fingers curling into my shirt, and kissed me back softly. Warmth exploded through my chest, and I seized her waist.

Why had I kicked my gift to her underneath the couch earlier? Why had I been so scared, so afraid that she'd leave me? She was … more than I could have asked for. The best damn thing that had ever happened to me.

Whispers erupted around us, and I slowly pulled away to see the kids had stopped playing with their toys to watch us. Sierra giggled and rested her head on my chest, staring at the children.

"Merry Christmas," she whispered breathlessly to me.

I pushed back even more tears building in my eyes. "Merry Christmas, love."

42

sierra

"SO," Heather said, sipping her champagne after Christmas dinner, "how was your day?"

I drew my finger across the rim of my glass and bit back a grin. "Good."

She arched her brow. "Just good? Steven didn't ask you anything?"

"No …" I glanced over at her. "What would he ask me?"

Heather stiffened and grabbed my hand, leading me all the way across the room and toward the leather couch near the floor-to-ceiling windows. We had just finished dinner with Michelle and her submissive as well as Hector, and I was feeling tired already.

She glanced over her shoulder at the brothers. "Hector said maybe Steven would …"

After sitting next to her, I furrowed my brow. "Would what?"

"Give you a contract."

"A contract for what?" I asked.

She gently scratched her forehead with her manicured nails. "To be his submissive."

I stared at her quizzically.

"Usually, in a BDSM relationship, you have a contract that clearly and legally outlines the boundaries of the dynamic," she said. "Apparently, Steven asked Hector for advice about contracts, which is something he'd never done before."

My lips curled into a frown. "Oh."

She sipped her champagne. "Maybe he's saving it for another day."

"Or another girl," I whispered, the words tumbling out of my mouth before I could even process them in my brain. I knew it wasn't true, but between this and Steven not *really* telling me what my diamond necklace was at first … it made me wonder.

But I didn't want to think about that right now. Today had been amazing.

"Excuse me?" Heather said, staring at me, completely pissed. "You'd better take that back, Sea. We both know that man is head over fucking heels for you. Don't you even *think* that there is another girl in the picture."

I laid my head back against the couch and stared behind me through the window. "I know, but …" My heart raced. I didn't know why I had been so jealous suddenly. Maybe it was because I was beginning to fall so hard for him.

Butterflies fluttered in my stomach.

He had seemed so good with the kids today.

So happy …

"But nothing," she said. "If that ever happened, you know I would be the first one to"—she made a snipping motion with her index and middle fingers—"chop off his … precious penis."

A giggle bubbled up past my lips. "I know."

"He's just waiting," she reassured.

"But for what?"

"Maybe he prefers … something else and isn't sure if you're ready for it," Heather said.

I chewed on the inside of my cheek. "What else could he be into? He's relatively open with me—at least about sex." Though with personal things, he was still a bit distant. And I mean, I understood why, but I didn't know the reasons for him …

Not wanting to make it official.

Heather moved closer to me on the couch and gently nudged my shoulder with hers. "I know you've wanted a family since what happened a few years ago, but don't be so hard on yourself. I don't even know Steven, but he seems really happy with you."

"What can it be? What do I need to fix about myself?"

"Nothing!" Heather said a bit too loudly. After recovering by throwing Steven, Hector, and Michelle a small smile, Heather cleared her throat and lowered her voice. "You don't have to change anything about yourself. He might just be into … something different. And there's nothing wrong with you both learning what you're into."

My eyes burned with tears. "I don't want to be with anyone but him."

Maybe I wasn't pleasing him the way I'd thought I was. He had needs. He couldn't just teach me the ropes forever and be happy about not getting what he desired in return. And if I didn't please him, then someone else would.

"What do you think he's into?" I whispered.

After shrugging, Heather looped her arm around mine and rested her head on my shoulder. "I don't know. You should talk to him about it. Hector is into some more punishment and discipline kind of stuff. It could be something darker that Steven hasn't shown you yet."

Punishment? Discipline?

I chewed on the inside of my cheek and caught Steven peering at me from the table with his siblings. Once I shot him a smile so he wouldn't worry about me, I glanced down at my lap and bit back a frown.

Was that what Steven really enjoyed? What if I couldn't take the punishment he wanted to give me? Would he break up with me? He seemed to like spending time with me. If he didn't, then he wouldn't have invited me to stay for Christmas break with him. But why couldn't he tell me honestly what the necklace meant? Why didn't he want to make things serious?

"Stop getting into your own head about this," Heather said.

"I'm not," I reassured.

"You totally are."

Once I finally gathered the courage to look over at Steven, I swallowed. "I'm not."

He hadn't seemed to take his eyes off me since the last time I'd pulled my gaze away, his curious eyes suddenly wide with worry. He excused himself from the table and walked over to us casually, but I could tell that something was wrong.

"Are you okay, love?" Steven asked, sitting next to me on the couch, his arm curling around my shoulders and his worried gaze on me. "You look like you're about to get sick or cry or ... *both* right now."

Heather glanced between us, sent me a smile, then walked over to sit with Hector, Michelle, and her submissive.

I turned a couple of inches toward Steven and straightened my back. "I'm great."

"You're a terrible liar," he murmured.

After shaking my head to tell him that I really was fine, I placed my hand on his knee. "We were just talking about the class," I said to Steven, nerves bubbling up inside me. "Are we going to ... have a Discipline class?"

I remembered, a while ago, Steven had told me that I wouldn't be able to *take* his discipline, so maybe this really was what he was waiting for. Maybe he wanted to be sure that I could handle all aspects of being his submissive before he asked me.

He stiffened, as if he hadn't expected my question. "Do you want a Discipline class?"

My stomach twisted, but I wanted to please him. I wanted him to want me, to *love* me. Nobody in this world had made me feel so good about myself and about my life in a very, very, very long time. With him, everything felt so ... right.

"Yes," I whispered because I would do anything to please him.

43

steven

"MERRY CHRISTMAS," Hector said, hand stretched out toward me.

I shook it to wish him farewell and walked with him and his submissive to the door. Sierra had fallen asleep sometime in the past hour after Michelle left with her toy. And Heather was barely awake, holding on to Hector's opposite hand, eyes fluttering closed.

"You did good this year with dinner. Would've made Mom proud," Hector said, glancing behind me at Sierra on the couch. "I know it's been hard on you since she passed. She was the only real person we all had. But now, you have Sierra."

After following his gaze, I smiled and nodded. "Yeah, but ..."

"But?"

"I didn't give her the contract," I said, upset with myself.

"Hey," Hector said, squeezing my shoulder, "you have time. Don't rush it."

"I should've," I said, shaking my head. "She gave me a present that ... meant more to me than any other present someone had given me before. And I chickened out on gifting her a simple contract."

"It's not just a simple contract," Hector said, releasing my shoulder and giving me a small smile. We didn't talk as much as I did with Michelle, but I was glad he was supportive. "My first time was hard too. There's a lot of trust you both have to put in each other. Don't get down on yourself. It'll happen."

Hopefully.

Heather stumbled beside him, and Hector picked her up and tossed her over his shoulder.

"I have to get this one home. Just don't wait too long, Steven. Don't want her thinking that you're using her. That's the worst that can happen."

After saying goodbye to him, I quietly shut the door behind Hector and Heather and walked over to Sierra slowly so I wouldn't wake her. She lay on my couch, her hand tucked underneath her head and strands of her brown hair in her face.

I wished that I could've thanked her privately after she brought me to see all those kids today, but when we had returned home, Hector and Michelle had already been waiting for us. I had completely lost track of time with Sierra.

Shifting on the couch, Sierra rolled over onto her back with her mouth wide open and small snores drifting from her nose. I bit back a chuckle at how cute she looked, sprawled out on my couch, dressed up after a long Christmas Day.

After fishing the present out from underneath the couch, I sat on the side of it and glanced over my shoulder at Sierra. I wanted to redo this morning over so many times and wished that I could've found my balls to give her this.

She had given me a present that I hadn't even known I needed.

"There's no way that I could ever repay you for what you've done for me, love," I whispered.

As her head drifted to the side, her mouth fell open another inch, and I smiled down at her, laying the present in my lap. Moonlight flooded into the room from the floor-to-ceiling windows, gleaming against her face.

"Thank you," I murmured, knowing that she couldn't hear me.

But I didn't want to wake her. She had seemed upset earlier, yet she couldn't tell me why. Maybe she had a stomachache from the food. Or maybe it was because she hadn't drunk anything all day besides that champagne at dinner.

My gaze shifted from her to the contract that sat in my lap. "I promise to give this to you one day soon." My chest bubbled with lightness, and I couldn't help the smile that broke out onto my face. "I want it to be special."

I stayed seated on the couch for a while longer. Part of me hoped that Sierra would wake up so I could give it to her now and so that we didn't have to wait. Sierra had shown up for those kids when she didn't have to, when they hadn't even expected her to. And I had to take a leap of faith that she'd do that for me when I needed her.

Once I convinced myself to stand, I headed to my office and placed the present on my desk. Then, I walked to the bedroom, laid out some clothes for Sierra, and pulled down the comforter.

When I returned to the living room, one of Sierra's legs was sprawled up on the back of the couch and her head was hanging off the side, her snores louder. Damn, today had really taken a toll on her, hadn't it?

"Where are we going?" she mumbled into the crook of my neck as I picked her up.

"To the bedroom."

She shifted in my arms and smacked her lips together, as if her mouth was dry. I contemplated waking her up completely to give her one last present for Christmas, but she began snoring on my chest again, so I let her be.

I kicked my bedroom door open with my toe and walked with her toward the bed, gently setting her down in the center of it. After pulling off most of my clothes, I dressed her in the clothes I'd set out for her and crawled into bed behind her.

Something about being with her felt so natural. I didn't have to try too hard or hide my past from her, like I had felt obligated to do with everyone else I met. Never once in my life had I felt like I truly had a home.

But being with her was the closest thing to it.

We could be in the car, in her dorm, or walking around Giant Eagle, and still, everything felt at ease. Between her smile, her laugh, and everything about this goddamn woman, I didn't think I would ever find someone else so perfect for me.

She turned all the way over and cuddled up against my chest, as if she had been waiting for me. Or maybe it was because she was used to me holding her like this now.

"You're the best thing to happen to me, Sierra," I whispered against her hair because I knew she was fast asleep. I placed my lips on the top of her head and gently drew my fingers up and down the sides of her bare arm. "And I know it for certain now. I love you."

44

sierra

"WHEN WE'RE FINISHED TONIGHT, I'm going to bring you to Alta," Steven murmured, his hand on my lower back while guiding me through the crowd of people at Radiant.

I hadn't expected there to be this many people here between Christmas and New Year's Eve, but people were horny.

"Won't it be too late?" I asked.

"They'll stay open for me," he murmured. "Besides, I have a surprise for you."

"A surprise?" I asked, eyes growing wide. "Really? What is it?"

"Ah, love, do you need to freshen up on what the word *surprise* means?" He chuckled, albeit a bit nervously, and loosened his tie a smidgen. Then, he cleared his throat and gently captured my chin in his hand, eyes glinting. "You'll get it if you're good for me tonight, okay?"

With the heat gathering inside my core, I pressed my thighs together and nodded. Nerves bubbled inside my belly at the thought of what I would have to do tonight. I had told Steven that I wanted a discipline class—mainly to fulfill his needs.

"Is tonight's class still Discipline 101?" I asked.

Another chuckle left Steven's mouth, this one more relaxed. "You really want to be punished, don't you?"

I pressed my lips together, averted my gaze, and nodded. "Yes."

While I might've been nervous, it was *definitely* because I wanted to be able to fulfill him completely and not because I was scared with what these punishments were going to be and how hard he'd make them … *kinda.*

After we walked into class together, Steven rummaged through the closet for some *tools* he'd punish me with while I sat at a desk, nervous as hell. Other students began filling the seats around me, and I couldn't swallow the fact that I … that I …

Didn't really want to do this.

At least not in front of everyone else. What if I started crying? What if Steven pushed me past my limits and I had to use the safe-word? That would be beyond embarrassing, not only because the class would be watching, but also because I would have let him down.

And I couldn't do that.

"There are many forms of punishment that you can give your partner or, if you're in a BDSM relationship, your submissive," Steven said, starting the class, his gaze on the other students and not on me. "Mental punishment, restrictive punishment, orgasm control, lectures, chores, and more. But today, I'll demonstrate bondage, paired with physical punishment."

Once his gaze traveled to me, he nodded to the front of the class. I slipped out of my seat, nerves zipping through my entire body. I couldn't back down now. I had asked for this, and I had to take it, no matter how hard he gave it.

"Remove your clothes, Miss Monroe," he said.

When my clothes were off completely, he fastened my arms to chains that dangled from the ceiling and then placed a bar between my ankles to keep them spread, so I stood in an X position in front of the entire class.

"Are you ready?" he asked, moving in front of me and tucking some hair behind my ear.

"Yes."

"Are you sure?" he continued, giving me a chance to back down. But I refused. I would show him that I could be his submissive.

"I'm sure."

Steven cleared his throat and headed to the main table that had all his tools of punishment spread out on it. I swallowed hard and glanced nervously from each one, wondering how hard he'd use them on me.

After Steven explained almost all of them to the class, he picked up the last one, which I didn't recognize. "This is an electric shock rod. It doesn't need to be used as punishment, but it will provide a slight shock to your partner."

A shock?

Steven is going to shock me?

He placed it down. "We'll use this toward the end of class."

The first toy he picked up was the crop.

"You can use this on many parts of the body, as the end is not as stiff as a paddle," he said, the flimsy side of it lying across his palm. He placed it against my belly and gently drew it up the center of my body to my face.

When the end met my cheek, he lightly tapped it, as if to get me used to the sensation. I stared up at him, pussy aching as a small smile creeped across my lips. This didn't seem too bad, to be honest.

All I was nervous about now was that electric shock rod.

He tapped it again, harder, against my cheek. I bit back a moan, the pleasure beginning to fill my body, and let him do it once more. I tried to pull my legs together, but the spreader bar around my ankles forced me to keep my legs apart.

Once more, he moved the crop further down my body and snapped it against my breasts, leaving a light pink mark. His eyes lit up with excitement as pleasure gushed between my legs. This was exactly what he liked, wasn't it?

Again. And again.

Then, he moved the crop further down, tracing my inner thighs. He pulled it a couple of inches away from my skin, then smacked it against my clit. I threw my head back and moaned, the sensation like nothing I'd felt before.

"This doesn't seem too much like a punishment," Steven hummed, placing down the toy.

After picking up the flogger that had thick black leather strands attached to it, he stood behind me and gestured toward the class. "You need to be a good distance away from your partner so the tails of the flogger don't whip around and smack her in front of her body. You should be connecting with her thighs or backside, like this …"

Suddenly, he whipped the flogger through the air and smacked it against my ass, not hard, but not softly either. I winced but took the smack easily. He paused for a moment, his gaze lifting to the side of my face.

"I suggest staying away from the kidney and spinal column area," he continued.

Another smack, this one a bit harder.

"Count for me, Miss Monroe."

"One," I said.

He smacked it against my ass again.

"Two."

Another smack, and heat began coursing through my body.

"Three."

He grabbed my chin from behind. "Good girl."

After setting down the toy, he picked up the next one—a paddle.

I wrapped my hands around the chains to brace myself for the pain. He stood behind me and smacked me harder than he had with the flogger. I yelped and jumped up in pain as my ass began stinging from the sensation.

When I didn't say my safeword, he smacked me again and again in repeated succession. I gripped the chains even harder, my legs beginning to shake and my knees wobbly. He didn't stop until my ass was hot and throbbing. Then, he placed it down on the table.

There was only one toy left, which was the electric shock rod.

And while everything up until now had been bearable, I stood with my wrists bound to chains that hung from the ceiling and my legs spread in complete fear. I had basically begged him for punishment, and now … now, I was scared.

Scared that I wouldn't be able to take the shocks.

Scared that he'd leave me because I wasn't good enough.

I had never been shocked like this before. How would it feel?

"It is completely safe to use as long as you're using it correctly," Steven said, picking up the electric shock rod and placing it a couple of centimeters from his forearm.

The shock echoed around the room. While he didn't flinch, I did, and he hadn't even touched me with it.

After giving the class a basic rundown on how to use the shock rod and then reiterating that they should consult a mentor before using the shock rod themselves, he walked over to me and smiled softly.

"Are you ready for your punishment, love?" he murmured in my ear.

"Yes," I said without showing any kind of fear.

He moved behind me and gently placed one hand on my shoulder, and then my ass stung. I yelped and leaped into the air, heart pounding and backside aching already.

I squeezed my eyes closed, the pain not subsiding.

Another shock, and I whimpered again.

"If I'm hurting you, safeword," he said, suddenly at my side instead of behind me.

I stared at him through teary eyes and shook my head, refusing to let the word leave my lips. I had asked him for this class to show him that I could handle anything that he wanted to do to me, not to safeword in the middle of it and embarrass myself.

"I'm fine, Professor Patton," I forced myself to say.

"Sierra …"

"Please continue," I said. "Or did you stop because you don't have it in you to—"

He zapped me again. Tears wavered in my eyes.

Fuck, that hurt.

I dropped my head so nobody could see the pain written all over my face. While he stood behind me and couldn't see my expression either way, he stiffened, his breath hitching against my bare shoulder.

Is this it? Is this really what he enjoys? How will I be able to handle this forever? It hurts worse than anything else has.

When I showed no sign of backing down or saying my safeword, even though my body ached and my heart pounded so loudly inside my chest that I could hear it in my ears, Steven zapped me again.

My legs wobbled as a stray tear ran down my cheek.

"Stand up tall, Sierra, and take your punishment like a good girl."

While my knees were faltering, I did my best to stand up straight. This was what he wanted, so I had to give it to him. I had to do this for him, so he'd want me just as much as I wanted him. So he'd choose me to be part of his family because we both had nobody.

Three strong zaps came in quick succession, and I cried out in pain.

"Unicorn!" My knees gave out for good, and I hung by my wrists from the restraints, tears running down my cheeks and sobs tumbling out of my mouth faster than I could stop them. "Unicorn! Unicorn! Unicorn!"

45

steven

"CLASS IS DISMISSED," I said, unbinding Sierra as quickly as I could. "Everyone, out. Now."

The students quickly dispersed into Radiant, and I grabbed Sierra's wrists before she could drop completely to the ground. Her body had seemed to give out. Or maybe I had pushed her far past her limits. Had she said her safeword quietly at first and I just hadn't heard it?

Sierra pulled herself away from me and hugged her body.

I ignored the pinch of pain from her sudden actions and crouched down in front of her. "Sierra, what hurts?"

No response.

"What do you need?"

A sob.

"Can I get you anything, love? Please talk to me."

When she still didn't respond, I grabbed a blanket from the closet and draped it across her shoulders, placing her on the couch on the side of the room. Once she curled up into a ball with some pillows, I went to grab a water bottle from the cupboard, only to realize that Michelle hadn't stocked it.

"Sierra, I'm going to grab you some water," I said, crouching next to her. "Okay?"

No response.

After jogging out into the hallway, I found Michelle walking back to her office. "Michelle!"

She glanced over her shoulder with a big smile that immediately dropped. "What happened?"

"I need water. Something." I tried to catch my breath. "Anything. Please."

"What happened?" she repeated.

"Sierra said her safeword. The scene ended. She's freaking out, and I don't know why. She won't say anything to me. I need to get her some water and maybe a spare change of comfortable clothes to take her home in."

"Is she still in the classroom?" Michelle asked.

"Yes."

"You go get water at the bar. Let me talk to her and try to calm her down," Michelle said, heading toward the classroom. "Then, I'll get her changed and to your car. Okay?" She offered me a small smile. "It's going to be okay."

While I didn't like leaving Sierra alone with anyone, I trusted Michelle to dress her and make sure that she was comfortable. Sierra had pulled away from me so suddenly, almost as if she were scared. And she wouldn't calm down with me around if she feared me.

Heaviness weighed on my chest as I grabbed water from the bar. *Does she fear me?*

"Steven," Michelle said, hand on my shoulder before I headed to the car where she had brought Sierra after tending to her, "are *you* okay?"

"I'm fine," I snapped, needing to bring Sierra home, where she felt safe.

Before I could run out of Radiant, Michelle grabbed my wrist and yanked me back. With a furrowed brow, she looked over at me and frowned. "If you need someone to talk to about this, I'll always answer the phone for you, okay?"

After taking a deep breath, I dropped my gaze and nodded. "Thanks."

Guilt rushed through my system. I shouldn't have pushed Sierra.

I slipped out of Michelle's hold and headed for the running car, where Sierra waited, curled up against the window with a bouncer from the club watching her. I nodded to him and slid into the driver's seat, immediately heading for home.

My hand tightened around the steering wheel. I should've stopped before she even said her safeword. I ripped off a piece of skin from my cheek, anxiously tapped my fingers against the wheel, and glanced over at her sobbing body in my passenger seat. I wanted to comfort her, but back at Radiant, she hadn't wanted me to touch her.

And, God, it fucking hurt.

She still sobbed quietly to herself when we made it back to my high-rise.

"I'm going to lose him. I'm going to lose him. I'm going to lose him," she choked out between her sobs, holding and making herself small in the corner of the elevator, strands of hair falling into her face. "I'm going to lose him."

"Who are you going to lose?" I whispered, feet from her.

I wanted to approach her, but she was completely turned away from me, as if she didn't want to speak to me at all. She glanced over at me through teary eyes, her chin quivering. And then she burst out into more tears, her body shaking uncontrollably.

Deciding that I couldn't stand here and do nothing, I closed the gap between us and wrapped my arms around her body, no matter how much she stood there, completely closed off to me. Her arms were crossed in front of her body to put space between us, but her head was on my shoulder.

Why hadn't she said her safeword sooner? I had made sure that she was comfortable with it many times over. I had *asked* her if she was okay in the middle of the scene, and yet ... she had refused to say it until it was too late.

"I'm giving you a bath," I whispered when the elevator dinged.

The doors opened on the top floor. I picked Sierra up and brought her into my high-rise. As the lights turned on automatically, I placed her down on the cushioned vanity chair and began the warm water, hoping it'd calm her down.

This had never happened to me before, and I loathed myself for it. I should've known her limits even better than I'd thought I did and should've stopped when I sensed something was wrong. I shouldn't have kept going, and because I had, we were in this position. Guilt rushed through me. This was my fault.

Once the tub filled up three-fourths of the way, I peeled off Sierra's clothes and gently placed her down into the bath. Instead of resting her head back against it and relaxing, she drew her knees to her chest and held them close, staring emptily at the soapy water.

"Are you okay?" I asked.

No response.

"Sierra," I said, moving my fingers toward her to push hair off her face.

She flinched away from me and reached behind her neck with her two hands. "Here," she said, pulling off her diamond necklace and handing it to me, as if she wanted nothing to do with it anymore.

Sorrow and regret seeped into my bones. *Sierra's breaking up with me?*

"What are you doing?" I whispered in pain.

"You already don't want me because I'm not a good enough submissive for you," she said, her voice cracking at the end, leading to another hoarse sob. "You're going to get rid of me the moment the semester is over. So, take it."

My eyes filled with tears. "What are you talking about?"

Did I not make her feel good or wanted in every class? I swallowed and pressed my trembling lips together. *Did I lead her to believe I would leave her for someone else? Did I stare at another girl in the club too long? Do something I shouldn't have?*

"I'm sorry that I can't please you the way you need," she said between sniffles. "You deserve to be with someone who can, Steven.

So, please stop acting like you like me. It's confusing me, and … and I …"

"Sierra," I whispered on my knees, leaning over the tub and taking her face in my hands. The water sloshed over the edge of the bath, wetting my pants. "What are you talking about? I love you. So much. What makes you think that you don't please me or that I don't want you?"

She stared at me through glossy eyes and wiped some tears with her knuckles. "You …" She hiccuped. "You what?"

Did those words really leave my mouth? Did I admit that I loved her?

She was a crying, sobbing mess and had just safeworded in front of me. How could I put something this huge on her right now? Would she even believe me? Was it wrong to tell her how deeply I felt about her?

No, she needed reassurance.

"I …" I paused. "I love you."

She scanned my face for a moment, and then she finally shook her head. "You're lying."

Her accusations fucking butchered me.

"I'm not lying to you," I whispered, lips quivering from her claims that weren't true. "I'm terrible at showing my feelings sometimes, Sierra. But I'm not lying to you. I wanted to give you a contract to be my submissive on Christmas morning, but I was too scared."

"Scared of what?" she asked, brow furrowed. "Of me?"

"Of losing you," I said, voice barely audible. "I can't lose you. I can't. I can't do it."

Another pause.

"You were really going to give me a contract?" she whispered. "You're not lying?"

God, I should've just done it on Christmas. I should've woken her up and given her the present. It would've prevented all of this from happening, would've prevented these tears and Sierra's terrible thoughts.

"Wait here," I said, hurrying to my home office and grabbing the matte-black box.

Once I returned to the bathroom, I sat down on the wet floor in front of her and handed her the box. "I'm sorry I didn't give it to you sooner."

She stared at it for a couple of moments, then uncapped the box and looked down at the agreement. More tears filled her eyes, and she suddenly handed me back the box. "If you don't want to give it to me, then you don't have to, Steven. I don't want to pressure you into it."

"You're not pressuring me into doing anything, love," I whispered, gently stroking her wet hair. "I promise you that I had been planning on giving you the contract tonight over dinner too. I wanted it to be special since I'd completely fucked it up on Christmas."

Again, her eyes filled with tears. "I ruined it."

"You didn't ruin anything," I whispered, not wanting her to feel even worse.

She wasn't in a good place right now, and putting something like this on her would make it even more terrible.

"How about we finish your bath and we can review the contract together over dinner? We can stay in and …" I offered her a smile. "Maybe you can teach me how to cook one of your family's recipes. Does that sound good?"

After looking back and forth between me and the contract, she eventually stared into my eyes and nodded softly. "Okay," she said, voice barely above a whisper. "That sounds good. As long as I'm not pressuring you into something that you don't want—"

"You're not," I reassured her, peeling off my shirt. "You got room in there?"

She wiped away the last of her tears with the backs of her hands and smiled softly at me. "I'm sure I can make some room."

46

steven

THE NEXT MORNING, Sierra and I sat on the couch together with the contract.

As soon as she had stepped out of the tub last night, she'd basically fallen asleep. I dried her off as she wobbled back and forth on her feet, then carried her to the bedroom. We still had so much to talk about, but I'd figured that she needed to rest.

Too much stimuli at once would only make things worse.

"You ready?" I asked.

She cuddled up next to me and placed her head on my shoulder. "Are *you* ready?"

"Yes."

Her lips turned down. "But you seem so tired. Did you sleep last night?"

I bit back a yawn. "A little."

Honestly, I had been awake for so long last night, hating myself for pushing her too far. I'd paced the living room so many times, wondering why I hadn't been clearer and more direct with her because she was so new to all this.

"Something's bothering you. What is it?"

"I'm sorry if I hurt you last night," I whispered, pushing some hair off her forehead.

She stayed quiet for a long time. "You didn't hurt me. I was just scared."

"But you shouldn't have even been scared, Sierra. I was the one who did that to you."

"It's my fault." She frowned. "Don't be sad."

"I can't stress enough how important it is that you say your safeword if you've reached your limit." I tucked some more hair behind her ear and tilted my head a couple of inches to the side. "If you keep it to yourself, then it breaks our trust."

She twisted her body on the couch toward me and frowned. "Did I break our trust?"

I grimaced because I didn't want her to feel bad about it and I wanted to stay with her, but I … I feared that I'd go too far again. That she'd *let* me go too far. And I would hurt her, physically or emotionally. And if I hurt her, then I'd hurt myself and our relationship.

"I did," she whispered, eyes watering as she curled her arms around herself. "I'm sorry."

"Just don't do it again, love, okay?"

Her chin quivered. "Okay."

After gently grasping it, I drew my thumb across her cheek. "Don't cry. It's not your fault. We both made mistakes. If I had been honest with you from the beginning, you wouldn't have thought you had to do anything for me."

"But still"—she sniffled—"I broke your trust. I didn't mean to."

Once I pulled her into my arms, I laid her head on my shoulder and rubbed her thigh. "I'm not scolding you. I don't want you to feel bad about it, but I want you to understand that you must use a safeword so I know that you're safe. The last thing I want to do is hurt you."

"Safewords are to keep us safe," she said.

"To keep both of us safe," I repeated, wanting to really make sure she understood. "If you don't say something and I push you too far, it hurts both of us. I don't want that to happen again, so let's give you another word before your safeword for when I'm approaching your limit, okay?"

"What is it?"

"Our caution word will be *yellow*," I offered. "And if you'd like to change *unicorn* to *red*—"

"I like unicorn," she said with a small giggle.

"Unicorn it is." I chuckled, grabbing the pen and contract from beside me and allowing Sierra to write her caution word and safeword on the blank lines. "Now, let's finally get to explaining what this all means for you, okay, love?"

She leaned back and curled up next to me. "Okay!"

Two hours and twenty-five questions later, Sierra leaned back on the couch with the contract in her hands. I was happy to address all her questions because that meant she could understand our dynamic more. I'd much rather her understand completely instead of having another episode like what had happened last night.

It'd hurt my heart to see her so freaking sad.

"I have another question."

"What is it, love?"

"So, will you tell me honestly if the necklace that you bought me is a collar?" she asked.

"Sierra—"

"You said we have to be honest with each other."

"I didn't buy you the necklace with the intention of using it as a collar. I bought it for you because, at the time, I felt about you in a way that I hadn't felt about anyone else before. I was scared of telling you how I felt and thought that a necklace would do it all for me."

For some reason, her face dropped. "Really?"

A low chuckle escaped my mouth. "Did you want it to be a collar?"

"Everyone kept saying it was."

While she had wanted me to be honest, there was no harm in telling her a little white lie, especially if that was what she wanted it to be. Maybe it really had been a collar, but *I* hadn't realized it. That wasn't something I had done with anyone else either.

"Maybe it is," I hummed, and her eyes grew wide with excitement. "Would you like that?"

Cheeks rounding, she bit back a smile. "Maybe."

"Maybe?"

"Definitely," she clarified, snatching the pen from me. "I'll sign the contract right now if you admit that it's a collar."

"You're not going to sign it today." I chuckled. "I want you to think about it and make sure that you truly understand what this means. Ask your friends to read it over, if you're comfortable with it. Heather's mom is a lawyer, right?"

"I can't ask her to look this over!" She scrunched her nose. "She's like a mom to me."

"All I'm asking is that you read it over a couple of more times then."

After she nodded, I flipped to the last page, which included a list.

"And here, at the end of the contract, is a list of kinks that I'm comfortable with." I handed her the pen. "I want you to circle, underline, or check all the kinks that you would like to explore and ones that you're already comfortable with."

She clicked the pen a few times, chewing on the inside of her cheek while staring down at all the kinks that I had marked myself. Finally, she pushed the pen onto the paper and marked the kinks off, one by one, until she reached the very end.

Her pen hovered over *Breeding*.

"Breeding?" she repeated. While her voice was soft, her nipples hardened underneath her shirt, making my dick stiff at the mere sight. She glanced up at me through innocent eyes. "Can you explain what that one means, *Sir*?"

47

BREEDING?

I pressed my thighs together and stared between the contract and Steven. *Does Steven want kids? Does he want his own family soon? Is that what breeding means to him? How soon does he want them?* I was still on birth control. He wouldn't rip it out of me, like I'd read book boyfriends doing in those crazy dark romance novels.

"Typically, breeding means …"

A giggle left my throat, and I leaned forward. "I know what breeding means, but what does it mean in *this* context, Sir? Does the thought of getting me pregnant with your child get you excited?"

He rubbed the back of his neck and glanced away. "I—I don't … what I mean is …"

My chest was light and bubbly. "It turns me on."

As if my words didn't register, he ran a hand down his pant leg. "I thought—what?"

"You heard me." I giggled. "Plus, I am not going to ever say that again out loud."

Steven's brown eyes darkened even more, and he pulled me onto his lap so I straddled his waist. His hard cock was nestled between my thighs. A wave of heat coursed through my body, my pussy pulsing.

"Breeding turns you on?" he asked.

"It definitely seems like it turns you on too. You're so hard."

A low growl—a noise that I had never heard Steven make—rumbled from his chest. I clenched, my nipples becoming even harder, and ground down against him. Through my oversize T-shirt, he seized my nipples between his fingers and squeezed them.

Just as Steven drew me in for a kiss, someone knocked on the front door. Steven pulled away slightly and glanced over at it, groaning slightly. After the knock came for a second time, he placed me on the couch beside him and readjusted his pants.

My lips curled into a smile. "You look excited."

"Don't get me started, love," he murmured, throwing me a glance.

"Expecting visitors?"

When he pulled the door open, Michelle grinned from the hallway and thrust a plate full of freshly baked blueberry muffins at him. "Good morning!" she said, walking right into the room and heading over to me. "I wanted to check in on you to see how you are."

Cheeks reddening, I fiddled with my sleeve. "I'm good. Sorry about last—"

"Oh, stop it!" she said, waving her hand dismissively. "I remember the first time I ever said my safeword in the middle of a scene. I was terrified and sobbed for hours afterward. Steven brought me muffins the next day because he had seen how torn up I was at the club." She beamed at him over her shoulder. "So, I thought I'd return the favor."

I smiled. "I didn't know he could cook muffins."

"He can't," she whispered loudly behind her hand, plopping down on the couch beside me and giggling softly to herself. "All the muffins were burned on the bottoms, but it was the thought that counted."

"That's so sweet." I giggled.

"Anyway," she said, rubbing my knee, "if you need to talk, you know where to find me. And if I'm on the floor at Radiant, just ask the front desk for me, and I'll come out to chat with you anytime. Okay?"

I nodded. "Thank you."

"Of course, sweetheart. So, what are your plans for—" Michelle stopped short when she spotted the contract on the coffee table. After eyeing it for a couple of moments, she glanced up at Steven, who had finished pouring her a cup of tea. "Never mind. I see you've both been busy."

After side-eyeing his sister, Steven handed her the tea.

"Oh, I am so excited!" She jumped up and hurried to the door with Steven's mug. "Well, I don't want to keep you both from … *things* … so I'm going to see myself out. Can't waste the tea. It's my favorite. I'll return your mug tomorrow. Toodaloo!"

The door slammed behind her, and then a moment later, she reopened it and ran over to Steven, patting him on the head. Yes, right on the head and a cute little pat, like you would with a boy. "I am so proud of you!"

And then she was off again.

We both waited for her to return, but she didn't this time.

Steven picked up the muffins from the counter and brought them over to me. "Why don't we hold off on any sexual endeavors for now? I don't want to push it so soon after last night." He handed me a muffin and pulled me off the couch, his hand smacking against my ass as he sent me down the hallway. "Get dressed. I have to pick up some groceries at Giant Eagle."

"*You*, going grocery shopping at my favorite store?!" I exclaimed, running down the hall. "Say no more!"

48

steven

AFTER SLIDING up onto the classroom desk, I collapsed my hands together and hoped that Sierra would show up today. She, Heather, and a couple of their friends had gone shopping at the mall for New Year's Eve dresses. But she'd seemed nervous when I mentioned another class.

To finish the class time that everyone had missed after Sierra said her safeword, I added another one a few days later onto our calendar and emailed the class that they could attend it if they were available.

I hadn't planned on a demonstration today because we had a far more important lesson.

To my surprise, the seats filled up in the classroom more than I'd thought they would for a last-minute addition. Every time the door opened, I raised my gaze and hoped that Sierra would trickle into the room tonight.

One minute before class officially began, all the seats were full, except hers. I frowned at the thought of Sierra not feeling comfortable in my class anymore since she had used her safeword, but reminded myself that she just needed time.

"Okay, let's get started." I cleared my throat. "Our class today won't be as long as usual."

Before I could officially begin, the door opened, and Sierra scurried into the classroom, like she had done for the first class after I told her not to be late. With her cheeks flushed, she slipped onto her seat. "Sorry I'm late, Professor."

"Don't let it happen again, Miss Monroe," I said playfully.

She bit back a giggle behind her grin, and I returned to the class.

"Most of you witnessed one of your classmates saying her safeword last class."

A couple of students glanced over at Sierra as she slouched down in her seat, turning her gaze to the top of her desk. This wasn't to embarrass her in any way or to shame her. But it was an example that everyone here had witnessed.

"A safeword is to alert your partner that you don't feel safe, that you're hurting, or that you'd like to stop the scene." I cleared my throat and looked around at the students. "There is no shame in ever saying your safeword. Understand?"

The students nodded.

"As soon as you hear your partner say his or her safeword, you stop." I paused to let it sink in for the rest of the students. "It doesn't matter what you're doing or how much pleasure something is giving you. To be a good partner, you stop immediately and ensure that your other is safe, physically, mentally, and emotionally."

"What happens after your partner says their safeword?" someone asked from the back.

"Sometimes, you might continue the scene after you've confirmed with your partner that they're okay. At other times, you will need to stop the scene for the night and begin aftercare immediately."

"Can you explain aftercare?" another student asked.

"Aftercare is a time after sex where you recover with your partner and tend to each other's needs. Showing that you care. Making sure they're okay. Helping them return to reality. It will be different for every couple, but it usually includes two elements—

physical and emotional. Physical involves removing any restraints, making sure they drink, and comforting them after a draining session. Emotional involves talking about the scene"—I glanced over at Sierra—"about your reasons for saying your safeword, and reassurance."

"So, cuddling?" a woman asked beside Sierra.

"Cuddling is a good example. I personally enjoy giving my partner warm baths to help her relax." I slid off the desk and walked around the front of the classroom. "You can also make warm tea or do something you both enjoy together."

"Is aftercare always needed?" she asked.

"Sometimes, your partner might not enjoy aftercare, so it's important to talk about your needs in the beginning of a relationship," I said because I hadn't really enjoyed receiving aftercare myself until Sierra. "Other times, your partner, who doesn't like aftercare, might really, really need it, and he or she doesn't even know it."

Sierra's lips curled into a small smile, and she tucked some hair behind her ear, so innocent and shy, like the first night I had met her. God, sometimes, I wished we could relive that night over and over again. But then I realized that being with her like this was so much better.

When nobody had any more questions, I moved on to the next subject.

"Next class, you'll choose a partner for an end-of-semester project." I glanced at Sierra, excitement running through my body, and drew my tongue across my inner teeth. "So, make sure to choose your partner wisely."

"What's the project, *Professor*?" Sierra asked.

My lips curled into a smirk. "Patience, Miss Monroe. Patience."

She kicked her legs back and forth underneath the desk, so innocent. She had no idea what I had in store for her in a few days. That woman had teased me about wanting to breed her, so I would. And she'd love every moment of it.

"Class is dismissed. If you have any more questions, feel free to ask after class."

As the students began walking out of the room, some lingered behind to ask questions about aftercare and safewords. And while we had talked about it earlier on in the semester, it was always great to have a refresher and learn more about it.

Once the remainder of the students left, Sierra sauntered over to me and slipped up onto my desk. I placed my hands on her knees and drew them up her thighs as I moved between her legs.

"I'm happy that you came today."

"Me too," she whispered, moving her hands around my shoulders. "So ..."

"So?"

"What can I do?"

I arched my brow. "Hmm?"

She poked me in the belly. "For you to tell me what this project is."

I cupped her face in one of my hands, leaned down, and chuckled against her mouth. "The only thing you need to know about the project is that it's a huge part of your grade. You'll get a chance to get an A-plus for the semester if you complete all aspects of it."

"Oh, yeah?"

"Yeah."

"And how do we get an A?"

Gently biting down on her lower lip, I sucked for a moment. "You'll have to wait and see."

49

sierra

"SO?" Heather said, leaning back against the balcony that overlooked Pittsburgh. She pulled her white fur coat over her shoulders and placed one of her red bottoms against the concrete wall. "Did you give him the contract back?"

"I want to do it when the time is right," I hummed, glancing into the party at Steven.

Steven and Hector chatted with each other over a glass of wine on the suede white couches at Alta for their New Year's Eve party. I glanced at Athena, who stumbled onto the balcony after flirting *heavily* with Charlie.

"You sure the contract looks good?" I asked Athena.

She threw her arm around my shoulders. "You literally haven't given it back to him yet?!"

Heather threw her hands into the air. "That's what I'm saying."

"The contract is perfection." Athena giggled, some of her shimmering black hair falling into her face. "I honestly don't think that a contract could be more in your favor. You can step away and cancel the contract whenever you'd like."

My chest filled with warmth as Steven glanced over at me from across the restaurant. I smiled back at him and gnawed on the inside of my cheek. Steven had given me ample time to review the contract, and *thank God* that Athena was going to law school because I would never have asked Heather's mom to review a contract like that. She'd judge me for days!

And maybe even be suspicious of Heather and Hector. I couldn't do my best friend dirty.

"Professor Big Dick is here," Heather hummed, pushing herself off the balcony and grabbing Athena's hand to drag her stumbling ass back into the restaurant. "Have fun out here! Make sure to give him a big ole smooch at midnight!"

Once they disappeared into Alta, I leaned against the balcony in Heather's place and watched Steven approach me slowly. He had that dark and lively look in his eyes and held out a glass of champagne for me.

"It's almost midnight, love," Steven murmured.

"That means I've gone almost eighteen hours, trying to guess what this huge project is."

He chuckled and lifted the glass to his lips. "And you still haven't gotten it correct."

I gently tugged on his tie to pull him closer. "Maybe you can give me a hint."

After setting his glass on the balcony behind me, he trapped me in with his arms on either side of my body and dipped his head, drawing his nose down mine, his lips hovering over mine. "You want a hint?"

"Mmhmm," I said, staring up into his eyes. "Pleeeeease."

Another low chuckle escaped his throat. "No."

"What?!" I exclaimed, gently pushing his shoulders. "You can't come over here, all sexy and playful, and *not* give me a hint! That is totally against all the rules."

"And what rules are those?" he asked in amusement.

"The law. Duh."

"In what country?"

I crossed my arms. "Mine."

"What other outrageous rules does your country have?"

"Firstly, my rules are *not* outrageous." I tilted my head, as if I were uninterested in the conversation anymore, and sipped my champagne. "But the second rule in the land of Sierra is that you—"

"Have to go to Giant Eagle with you at least once a week?" he hummed.

My mouth dropped open. "How'd you know?"

"Lucky guess." He chuckled, tilting my head back toward him and gliding his thumb across my lower lip.

I almost expected him to push it into my mouth, so I swiped my tongue across it like a dumbass, my cheeks flaming in embarrassment when he didn't.

"Good girl."

I poked him hard in the chest. "That's another rule. No doing that."

"No doing what?"

"What you just did!"

"You'll have to be more specific, love."

"Teasing me."

"Teasing you? I'm doing no such thing. I'm rewarding your behavior with praise."

Heat coursed through my body. "You know what that does to me."

A small chuckle left his mouth as he dropped his lips to my ear. "Now, I *really* need you to be more specific. How does me calling you a *good girl* affect that pretty little pussy, love? Does it make it all warm? Does it get it all tight and wet for me?"

"No!" I exclaimed, becoming more flustered by the moment. "It does not!"

"Are you sure about that? Your thighs are pressed together, trembling."

When his fingers gently brushed against my thighs that I certainly had pressed together, I sucked in a breath and stared up into those big brown eyes. "And what if it does? What're you going to do to me?"

"Reward you," he hummed.

My nipples hardened underneath my silky dress, catching his attention. He gently captured one between his fingers and tugged.

"What a good girl you are for me tonight."

From inside Alta, our friends began counting down from ten, staring at the television, which played the infamous broadcast of the ball dropping in New York City. I curled my fingers around Steven's collar and drew him closer.

"I'll always be your good girl," I murmured against Steven's lips.

"Always?" he asked, resting his forehead against mine.

"Always."

"Three!" they shouted from inside the restaurant. "Two! One!"

I pulled Steven closer and closed the distance between us, crashing my lips onto his, making a new tradition to kiss him every New Year's on midnight. I had never experienced a New Year's Eve kiss before, and by the way Steven wrapped his arms around my waist and spun me in the air, his lips on mine, it didn't seem like he had either.

But it'd be a new tradition that we'd add on to our ever-growing list.

50

sierra

"IN TODAY'S CLASS, you'll choose a partner that you'll be working with for the rest of the year," Professor Patton said, grabbing a piece of chalk and writing *Breeding 101* on the board. "I'll demonstrate how to breed your willing partner."

I tightened and stared at him through wide eyes.

Breeding? Does that mean … am I …

He placed the chalk down and gazed at me, his dark eyes filled with hunger.

This is what he was hiding from me?

His gaze dropped to my tits, then even lower to my stomach. "And my lovely partner, Sierra, will show all the ladies how to take two balls' worth of warm cum in her cunt today."

Heart pounding inside my chest, I clenched. He had filled me with his load of cum countless times before today's class, but never once had he given me this … *look* that he was giving me now.

Hunger to intentionally come inside me.

Desire to … to …

After I swallowed hard, I pressed my thighs together. I couldn't even allow myself to think of what he wanted to do to me. I was sitting in his Breeding 101 class, knowing exactly his intentions, but unable to get them through my head.

And one day, it would actually happen.

"You'll have the next two weeks of classes off, but you and your partner will be working together on a final project outside of school. You will use what you learned this semester," Professor Patton announced, then turned his gaze on me again. "And if you get a woman pregnant or get pregnant by the end of the semester, you'll receive an A-plus for the class."

Warmth exploded through my core, and I curled my toes.

Pregnant. Professor Patton wants to make me pregnant.

Fuck. Fuck. Fuck. Fuck. Fuck.

Wetness gushed between my thighs, and I gripped my desk until my knuckles turned white. This class wasn't on the syllabus. We hadn't even learned anything about breeding within the textbook. Had he added this class ... just for me?

I clenched again, my panties soaked through already.

No, he couldn't have. I'm sure it is on the syllabus, and I just missed it. Right?

It wasn't because I'd mentioned that I wanted him to breed me, was it?

"Sierra," he beckoned, walking to a gray ottoman that stood between his desk and the first row of student desks, "come up here and remove your clothes. You're going to show everyone how much of a willing partner you are."

Scurrying up to the front of the class, I gulped and stared at the students. Stripping my clothes in front of all these men and women still hadn't become easier at all for me, but I couldn't help myself when it came to Professor Patton.

After pulling off my shirt and shimmying out of my skirt, I stood in a lacy pair of black lingerie. My nipples poked against the material, hard and aching to be tugged. And my panties ... God, my panties were already soaked.

"Turn toward me," Professor Patton ordered.

Twirling around, I stood in front of him and unclipped my bra.

The straps slipped down my shoulders, and the bra fell off me. I pressed my thighs together and stared up at him, nipples hardening even more from the sudden chill in the air.

Professor Patton's gaze traveled down my body to my tits, lingering. He reached out and seized my nipples between his large fingers, pulling me forward. A rush of heat exploded through my core, and I whimpered.

"Your panties too," he said.

While he still held my tits, I pushed my underwear to the ground. After pinching my sensitive buds once more, he released them, crouched in front of me, and picked up my thong.

"You're not going to need these for the rest of the semester."

He nodded to the ottoman.

"On your stomach. Legs together."

I lay on my stomach with my thighs pressed together and looked back at him

Once Professor Patton undid his buckle, he stripped his shirt and stepped out of his pants, his muscular, taut body on display. The overhead light created shadows on his shoulders and biceps, making him look even bigger and stronger. My pussy clenched at the sight of him.

Breed.

Professor Patton was going to breed me.

He had been inside me countless times before, but him being inside me during this session would be different. Professor Patton would be actively trying to get me pregnant.

When he crawled up onto the cushion with me, he straddled my legs from behind, his cock brushing against my ass cheeks. I clenched and shimmied my ass up a couple of inches so he'd be able to slip right into my wet pussy.

I needed him inside me so badly.

"Lift your ass up further," he ordered, gently tugging up on my hips.

After I lifted my hips, Professor Patton placed a pillow next to me and slid it underneath my hips, so I didn't strain my lower back.

With my ass in the air, he inched closer to me and rubbed the head of his cock against my glistening pussy lips.

"You're not on birth control, right?"

"I am," I whispered. "I have an IUD."

Jaw clenched and gaze hardening, he drew his tongue across his teeth and quietly growled. "After this class, we're going to fix that," he said. "You do want to earn an A-plus for the semester, don't you?"

"Y-yes, I do!"

"Good girl." He drew his nose up the back of my neck. "So willing to be bred."

Desperate for him to thrust himself inside me already, I arched my back harder and lifted my ass further into the air, grinding my pussy against the head of his dick. I gripped on to the pillow, furrowed my brow, and closed my eyes.

"Please," I whispered.

God, I needed it so badly. My pussy ached to be filled.

"I'm not going to stop until you take every last drop of my cum tonight," he said, leaning down further and lowering his voice to continue speaking to me and only me. "And every night until the semester is over. We're going to get you that A-plus, love."

He pushed the head of his huge cock into me. Inch by inch, he sank further inside me, spreading my pussy lips apart and filling me with his long, thick shaft. I curled my toes and clutched his dick.

When the base of his dick met my pussy lips, he paused. His heavy balls grazed against my clit, his hands clutching my ass cheeks and pulling them apart. I clenched harder around him, aching for him.

"Fuck, Sierra," he growled. "I can't wait to fuck you pregnant."

And then he drove himself into me over and over. I grabbed the side of the ottoman, curling my fingers into the cushion and moaning wildly. I could feel every inch slide in and slide out, my pussy desperate when it was empty. Every time he thrust into me, it somehow felt like he rammed deeper.

Pressure rose in my core. He hadn't been inside me for more

than a few minutes, but pleasure surged through my body. If he kept this pace up, I would ... I would ... God, I was going to come undone already.

After he rested one hand on the cushion beside me, he grabbed a fistful of my hair with his free hand and lifted it so I looked up at him. "After you come, you're going to beg for me to get you pregnant. Do you understand?"

"Yes, Professor," I whispered.

He flipped me around so I lay on my back and my legs rested on his shoulders. Pleasure soared through my body. After placing his hands on either side of my torso, he plunged himself back into me, getting even deeper this time.

I clenched around him and moaned, my pussy lips gripping on to his throbbing cock.

"I've never done anything with a student before you. You do something to me, love," he growled. "Something so intense that I'm now pounding you into this fucking ottoman and vowing that I'll put a baby in your stomach by the end of the semester."

"Don't stop," I begged, a whimpering mess.

My mind was empty of every thought, except ... *breed.*

Breed.

Breed.

I needed him to breed me.

He couldn't stop. He couldn't pull out. He needed to come inside me.

"I'm going to breed you every night," he started, shoving his cock deep inside me. "Until the fucking morning, until your tits and belly are round, until you're growing my fucking baby inside you, Sierra. You're mine now."

Pleasure exploded through me. My body jerked up, my pussy pulsing around his throbbing dick. I gripped his shoulders, desperately dragging my nails down his back.

"Please, come inside me!" I pleaded, pleasure rushing through me. "Get me pregnant!"

"Your pussy is gripping my dick so tight, like it's going to tear it fucking off," he hissed, pounding inside my sopping cunt. He gripped on to my shoulders and used my body to get deeper inside me, pulling me toward him with every thrust. "You want my cum that bad, don't you?"

"I don't want it," I whimpered, sinking my nails into his back muscle. "I need it. Please!"

"Sierra," he growled, almost as a warning that he was about to explode inside me.

And it only made me more desperate for his cum. I wanted every last drop of him inside me, like he had promised. I wanted him to shove it deeper and deeper and deeper until it reached my cervix, until he made me pregnant.

"Please come. Please come. Please come!" I breathed heavily. "I need it. God, I need it so badly. Make me pregnant, Professor Patton. I know you've wanted to since the moment I walked into your class. Please, make me—"

Professor Patton grunted deeply into my ear, "Fuuuuck."

His groan was nothing like I had ever heard before, like a savage animal that had lost all control. He grabbed me by the shoulders and ruthlessly began pounding into me, his cock getting deeper with every stroke as he growled huskily into my ear.

He shoved his cum deeper inside me until his balls were empty. And when he finally pulled out, he stayed hovering over me, his chest heaving up and down and his dark eyes fixed on mine.

"After you come inside her," he said breathily to the class while staring at me, "you're going to fuck her again. And again. And again." He continued, as if he were promising me that he'd be inside me again tonight, "And then again."

51

steven

A COUPLE of days after Breeding 101, I sat in my home office while Sierra showered in our bedroom after another round of me desperately trying to put a baby inside her. I scratched the back of my head and wondered if she considered it our bedroom yet. And, hell, a baby? My lips curled into a small smile. I surely hoped she wanted it as much as I did.

Even though another semester had started for Sierra, she hadn't returned regularly to her dorm. Instead, she had stayed over longer than I'd expected her to. And while I loved her here with me, I hated how she had been so quiet lately.

I leaned back in my chair and gazed out the windows that overlooked Pittsburgh. The sun had begun setting behind the buildings, pockets of light beaming out around the skyscrapers. I blew out a low breath and wondered if Sierra would stay with me forever here.

Someone knocked at my door.

"Steven, can we talk?" Sierra asked shyly, peering into my office.

I strolled over to her from my desk. "Of course we can, love."

With her hands clutching the contract, she twirled on her heel and headed toward the living room. I followed after her, my heart pounding inside my chest and my teeth gnawing at my inner cheek. It had been two whole weeks since I had given her the contract. And she hadn't said anything to me.

For a while, I'd thought she had forgotten all about it. I had urged her to take her time reading and understanding each and every section, but I had been tearing myself apart every night, wondering what her answer would be.

As she lingered by the couches, waiting for me to catch up with her, I noticed her diamond necklace lying on the coffee table. I sucked in a low breath and swallowed all those insecurities that had haunted me for years.

She sat down on the couch, grabbed the necklace, and handed me both of the items that I had given her because I loved her. My mouth was dry, and I couldn't help but feel like she had thought this all over and decided that it wasn't for her.

Even so, that wouldn't change the way I felt about her.

"I've thought a lot about the contract, Steven," she whispered.

Since the contract wasn't as important as she was to me, I laid it in my lap and gave her my full attention, offering her a small, supportive smile. "It's okay, love. I know this is all new to you. We don't have to move forward with anything that you're not comfortable with."

She stared at me quizzically for a couple of moments, and then a smile broke out onto her face, followed by one of her infamous, contagious giggles. "If you'll just flip to the last page already, you'll see that I can't wait to be your submissive, *Sir*."

I flipped to the last page to see her signature on the line with a small heart next to it. My lips curled into a smile, cheeks rounding and heart pounding inside my chest. This was … she really …

"Now, come here and collar me." Another giggle escaped her mouth as she crawled closer to me and sat on my lap. "A private lesson is needed to put me in my place. I've been a bad girl, Mr. Patton, for sleeping with my professor."

Join my newsletter to read the Epilogue, plus a bonus class, here.
Bound to My Father's Best Friend **is the next book in this series.**
Read it here.

also by emilia rose

Contemporary Romance

Stepbrother

Poison

The Bad Boy

Detention

Excite Me

Mafia Boss

Mafia Toy

Paranormal Romance

Submitting to the Alpha

Come Here, Kitten

My Werewolf Professor

The Twins

Four Masked Wolves

Monster Lover

about the author

Emilia Rose is a USA Today bestselling author of steamy romance. She loves writing about dirty-talking bad boys who are obsessed with innocent, and sometimes insecure, virgin heroines. She currently lives in a small town in Connecticut USA with her husband and three playful cats.

Join Emilia's newsletter for exclusive giveaways, early chapter releases, and more!

also by emilia rose

Scan the QR code with your phone to view all of Emilia's books!

www.ingramcontent.com/pod-product-compliance
Lightning Source LLC
Chambersburg PA
CBHW022130310726
48972CB00007B/2273